AMBER
AND
THE ENCHANTED
SWORD

....

MILTON J. DAVIS

MVmedia, LLC
Fayetteville, GA

MVmedia, LLC
PO Box 143052
Fayetteville, GA 30214
www.mvmediaatl.com

Publisher's Note: This is a work of fiction. Names, characters, places, and incidents are a product of the author's imagination. Locales and public names are sometimes used for atmospheric purposes. Any resemblance to actual people, living or dead, or to businesses, companies, events, institutions, or locales is completely coincidental.

Book Layout ©2017 BookDesignTemplates.com

Ordering Information:
Quantity sales. Special discounts are available on quantity purchases by corporations, associations, and others. For details, contact the "Special Sales Department" at the address above.

Amber and The Enchanted Sword/ Milton J. Davis. -- 1st ed.
ISBN 978-1-7346279-7-8

Contents

To Cammy, Alayna, Julian, and Ivy

Love cannot be divided.

—Kenyan proverb

CHAPTER ONE

Amber and Bissau sat face to face staring at the tennis ball in Amber's palm. They were alone on the Clifton Academy soccer field bleachers, the fall sky dotted with wispy clouds. Bissau's deep brown face was tight with concentration, but Amber's emotions were less focused. Her gaze kept drifting to Bissau's eyes, light brown irises with flecks of gold. He had the prettiest eyes she'd ever seen for a boy.

"Amber," Bissau said.

"What?" she replied.

"You're supposed to be concentrating on the ball."

Amber jumped. "Yeah, that's right."

She turned her attention back to the ball, her forehead furrowed with wrinkles.

"This isn't working," she said.

"It would, if you focused," Bissau replied.

Amber wrapped her fingers around the ball, drew her hand back then threw the ball by Bissau's head. It bounced off the bleacher seats, across the track, then onto the soccer field.

"It's not my skill," she said. "You said everyone is blessed with a certain nyama. Apparently, levitation is not mine."

"It is," Bissau said. "You have to practice."

"Why do you believe so much?" Amber said.

"Because Master Jakada said it is in your capacity," Bissau answered.

"Master Jakada could be wrong."

Bissau gasped. "Master Jakada is never wrong!"

Amber shrugged. "There's a first time for everything."

"I'm not going to sit here and listen to you insult Master Jakada," he said. "I have soccer practice soon. I'll see you later."

Bissau picked up his books, then sauntered away. Amber watched him with mixed emotions. This was not the way it was supposed to be. She expected things to be tough at her new school, and it was. Making new friends had not been easy; her classmates and some of her teachers were upset by her presence and expected her to be behind the curve coming from a public school. She proved them wrong, which seemed to make them more upset. Nothing like seeing your certainty smashed into little pieces, she guessed. And then there was soccer. The girls on her team had played together most of their lives. They were familiar with each other's strengths and weaknesses. Amber was an unknown, and none of them seemed eager to get to know her. Except Britani. The tall, lanky junior seemed out of place on the field, but she possessed a natural grace that reminded Amber of Jasmine. The rumor was Britani was a soccer phenom from Puerto Rico. Maybe that was why she took to Amber. She wasn't threatened by her. Amber rubbed her temples. All this thinking was making her head hurt.

"Amber, catch!"

Amber looked up to see Bissau throwing the tennis ball to her. She caught it.

"Keep practicing," he said before turning and walking away.

Amber opened her hand, then focused on the tennis ball.

"Rise up, stupid ball," she whispered.

The tennis ball shimmered against her palm, then launched upward like a round rocket into the clouds. Amber's eyes went wide with shock and glee.

"Hey, Bissau!" she shouted. "Hey!"

She jumped from the bleachers, running after Bissau.

"Bissau! I did it!"

Bissau turned about, a smile on his face.

"Where is the tennis ball?"

Amber pointed up.

Bissau's smile faded.

"How high?"

Amber shrugged. "I don't know. The moon, maybe?"

Bissau smiled. "I knew you could do it, but you must learn how to control it."

Amber folded her arms across her chest.

"I'm still trying to figure out why you're so-called training me. Let me see you levitate a ball."

Bissau sighed. "You know I can't. I need to go, and you do, too. We'll talk about it tomorrow."

"Whatever," Amber said.

She trudged to the girls' soccer field. Her teammates straggled in, talking and jibing each other. Their conversations diminished as Amber approached.

"Hey, Amber!"

She turned to see Britani jogging toward her, a soccer ball under her arm. Amber forced a smile to her face.

"Hey, Britani!"

Britani raised a hand for a high five and Amber obliged. She knew then what bothered her about Britani. She was trying too hard.

"What's up, gurl?" Britani asked.

"Same old same old," Amber replied.

Britani sucked her teeth. "I know that's right. Ready to show these kittens how to play football?"

Amber grinned despite herself. She was really trying not to like Britani.

Britani opened her arm, dropping the ball. She kicked it up, then kneed it to Amber. Amber bounced it back with her head.

"Hey," Britani said. "What's up with you and Bissau? Y'all like cousins or something?"

Amber stiffened and almost missed her turn passing the ball.

"We're friends," she replied.

"Friend friends, or girlfriend boyfriend?"

Amber hesitated. Why, she didn't know.

"Friend friends . . . I guess."

Britani frowned. "Don't be guessing. I need to know."

Amber cut her eyes at Britani.

"Why?"

Britani rolled her eyes.

"You need to ask? That boy is cute, and fine."

"And a bit short for you," Amber replied.

"I'm not complaining, and I know he won't."

Amber kicked the ball hard. It zoomed over Britani's head.

"Sorry," she said. *Not sorry*, she thought.

Britani trotted to retrieve the ball as Amber strolled to join the others. She ignored the tepid smiles and greetings of her teammates.

"Robinson," Coach Sandalwood called out.

Amber turned her head toward the coach. Mary Sandalwood was a stocky built woman with short cut red hair and pale freckled skin. In her youth she'd been a no-nonsense defensive player and had the distinction of playing on the US Olympic soccer team, as well as a few years as a pro in Europe. Her personal style of play reflected in the team. They were known for their impenetrable defense and straightforward offense; a direct opposite of the style Amber was used to playing. Amber adapted, but it was obvious the coach had little use for her skills.

"Yes Coach?"

Coach Sandalwood attempted to smile, which was like watching a snake try to shake hands.

"I want to try something different today," she said. "I want you to play defense."

Amber's mouth dropped open.

"Defense? I haven't played defense since elementary school!"

"So, you have some experience, then."

"Uhm . . . no!"

The coach cradled her tablet against her chest.

"You're a great player, very versatile," she said. "You know defense is our strength, and I only ask the best players."

"What about Cynthia?" Amber asked.

"Cynthia's a great forward," the coach said. "But she doesn't have your versatility. You would make our defense impenetrable."

"How do you know?" Amber asked. "Like I said, I haven't played defense since elementary school."

"Trust me," the coach replied. "There's a reason I'm the best soccer coach in the state."

Amber was proud of the fact that she didn't roll her eyes. The truth was Cynthia Hollingsworth was the face of the Wildcats. Everyone loved to watch her sprint up and down the field, her blond ponytail bouncing behind her as she dribbled the ball with imperfect precision to barely score. After the game the local media gathered around her, marveling at her 'skills' and predicting her amazing college and pro career to come. But there was no fighting it.

"Okay," Amber surrendered. "I'll give it a try."

"Carole!" the coached called out.

Carole Simpson strolled up to the coach. The straw blond-haired girl was their best defensive player, destined to receive accolades for her abilities.

"What's up, Coach?" Carole said in her syrupy southern drawl.

"Sit this scrimmage out," the coach replied. "Amber's playing your position."

Carole's eyes widened, then narrowed as she glared at Amber.

"She's not defense," Carole said.

"She is today," the coach replied. "Sit."

Carole gave Amber a hard stare before trudging to the bench.

Thanks coach, another enemy, Amber thought.

Coach Sandalwood sat down her tablet, then blew her whistle.

"Okay everyone, let's hard scrimmage!" she shouted. "First team!"

The coach looked at Amber.

"That's you, Amber."

Amber lowered her head, then rolled her eyes as she jogged onto the field. Not only was she being forced to play defense, Coach Sandalwood was having her play with the first team. The other players were looking at her with disdain while hand gesturing with Carole on the bench. Everyone except Britani. She threw up a peace sign.

"Alright now woman!" she shouted. "Let's see what you got!"

The scrimmage began. Amber felt useless as she waited in the back field for the action to come her way. It didn't take long. Britani worked her way down the field with her usual style, trailed by Cynthia. The two displayed great dribbling; Amber had to admit Cynthia was better than she gave her credit for. They maneuvered toward Amber, challenging her off the rip. Amber backpedaled until she knew who was going to go for the goal. As she suspected, Britani passed to Cynthia for the shot. Amber was halfway to her before Britani kicked the ball in her direction. Amber intercepted the pass as a mischievous smile came to her face.

"Time for some real practice," Amber said.

She kicked the ball hard. It soared high as Amber reached out for it with her nyama. She guided the ball over everyone's head to the opposite goal, catching the goalie off guard. But Penny Rothchild was good. She adjusted, diving for the incoming ball, her body extended and hands outstretched. Amber gave the ball a nudge and it just cleared Penny's hands. It hit the ground just before the goal then rolled into the net. Everyone froze in stunned silence.

"Damn!" Britani shouted.

"Language!" the coach replied.

Amber grinned as she strolled back to her position.

"Lucky kick," she said to the coach.

"Obviously," the coach replied.

Amber was rewarded by the astonished looks from her teammates. The rest of practice was as normal as practice could be with Amber playing defense. She didn't do as bad as she thought she would; Cynthia and Britani took advantage of her rusty skills, but Amber held her own at times. As practice came to an end Amber noticed the impressed looks on everyone's faces. The coach trotted up to her, a grin on her face.

"Not bad," she said.

"This isn't going to be permanent, is it, Coach?" Amber asked.

"No," the coach replied. "You're still a forward. It's good to know we could use you if injuries forced us."

Amber smiled. She'd dodged that bullet. She trotted to the locker room; Britani came up beside her.

"Look at you!" she said. "Playing defense like a beast!"

Amber smirked. "What can I say? I'm good like that."

Amber changed quickly then headed for the parking lot. She never knew which of her parents would be available to pick her up, but someone would be waiting. She met Bissau on the way to the lot. He was frowning.

"What's up? Something go wrong in practice?"

"No," he said. "Why did you do that?"

"Do what?"

"That kick?"

Bissau took out his phone, the screen filled with her 'miraculous' goal.' It already had over a thousand likes.

"Wow," Amber commented. "Lucky shot, huh?"

"You and I both know that had nothing to do with luck."

They reached the parking lot. Neither of her parents had arrived, so they sat on the curb to wait.

"Amber, you must take this seriously. You've been granted powers that have to be respected."

"I thought you'd be impressed," Amber said.

"Actually, I am," Bissau replied. "It didn't take you long to learn control. Why do you think that was so?"

Amber shrugged. "I don't know. I was pissed that coach put me on defense."

"So, your emotions help you control your nyama. That could be good and bad. I must consult Master Jakada about this."

"And just how to you do that?" Amber asked. "And why is he not talking directly to me?"

Bissau looked uncomfortable. "It's complicated."

Amber folded her arms. "Try me."

"Amber! Bissau!"

Britani fast walked up to them. Amber dropped her head and sucked her teeth.

"This thirsty girl," she whispered.

Britani sat down beside Bissau.

"How was practice?"

"It was good," Bissau replied. "And yours?"

"It could have been better, if Amber didn't ruin it."

"Don't blame me," Amber said. "It's the coach's fault. And you should play better."

Britani let out a girlish giggle and Amber sighed.

"So, Bissau, what are you doing . . ."

"Amber!"

Amber exhaled with relief as Mama rolled up in her SUV, waving like she hadn't seen Amber in years. But that was Mama. Amber jumped up, grabbed Bissau's arm and began dragging him toward the car.

"We'll see you Monday!" she said to Britani. She opened the back door then shoved Bissau inside the car.

"Uh, okay. Bye Amber. Bye Bissau!"

"That was rude," Bissau said.

"She was rude," Amber replied. "Busting up into our conversation."

"She was trying to be friendly. You are friends, aren't you?"

"She was talking to you, not me."

Bissau stopped. "What are you talking about?"

Amber shook her head. "Never mind."

Amber took the front passenger seat. She hugged Mama and Mama kissed her cheek.

"Hey, baby."

'Hey Mama."

"Hello Mrs. Robinson," Bissau said.

Mama turned and shared her famous smile with Bissau.

"Hi Bissau! How was your day?"

"It was good, Mrs. Robinson. And how was yours?"

"Excellent as always," Mama replied.

She looked at Amber. "Such a polite young man."

"Yeah, he's perfect," Amber grumbled.

Mama pulled away from the curb and they left the campus. Amber spotted Britani waving. Amber slumped in her seat.

"Baby, your friend is waving at you," Mama said.

"I know," Amber replied. "This ain't middle school."

"You can be so mean sometimes."

"I'm not mean, I'm honest."

"That's what mean people say."

Amber kept quiet the rest of the ride to Bissau's apartment complex while Bissau and Mama chatted. She was in a bad mood, but couldn't put her finger on why. So many things were happening that she didn't like, but she was usually able to handle it all. But for some reason, she was finding coping more difficult. She needed to talk to Jasmine. A silly conversation with her best friend always made her feel better. She'd text her as soon as she got home.

Mama pulled up into Bissau's complex. This was another mystery that needed solving. Bissau lived alone. Who was paying the rent? How was he able to get enrolled in the Academy

17

without his 'parents' permission? She'd asked him more than once, but he didn't answer. And he would never let her visit. They always studied at her house, the library, or the Starlight Coffee Shop.

Bissau grabbed his backpack and exited the car.

"Thank you again, Mrs. Robinson. I hope you have a wonderful evening."

"Goodbye, Bissau. Tell your parents I said hello. I hope to meet them one day!"

Bissau's pleasant façade cracked, but only for a second.

"I hope so too, Mrs. Robinson."

Bissau hurried up the walkway to his apartment. Mama waited until he was inside before pulling away.

"Such a nice boy," she commented.

"Yeah, he is," Amber replied.

"So, you two are friends?"

Here we go, Amber thought.

"Yes, Mother, we're friends. Just friends."

"That's how it starts," Mama said. "You know, me and your father were friends before we started dating, and now here we are!"

"Well, Bissau and I are really friends," Amber said. "You and pop were just pretending."

"But you're not best friends," Mama said.

"No. We're not best friends."

"You could do worse," Mama said. "Much worse. I mean, he's a good-looking boy, always neat, he's polite and he wears his pants up to his waist."

"I don't want to talk about this," Amber said.

"Okay, baby girl. Turn on some music. Some good music."

For Mama, 'good music' meant old music. Amber turned on the system. Mama's phone connected and a song by Prince played. Amber relaxed. She didn't like much old school music, but Prince was cool.

"Why didn't Dad pick me up?" she asked.

"Last minute meeting," Mama replied. "You know how it is."

She did. The good opportunities Mama and Dad received two years ago were a double-edged sword. One the one hand there was more money; on the other hand, there was less together time. As much as they got on her nerves, she loved them both and enjoyed spending time with them. While her other friends were doing everything in their power to distance themselves from their parents, Amber still liked sitting at the kitchen table with her parents or going on vacation with them.

Dad's car was in the driveway when they pulled up. The smell of garlic bread seeped into the garage and Amber's stomach grumbled.

"Somebody's hungry," Mama said.

Amber laughed. "Yes, I am!"

She opened the door. Daddy was at the stove stirring the spaghetti sauce, dress shirt sleeves rolled up and his tie tucked inside his shirt.

"Hey Daddy!" Amber said. She tipped to him and hugged him around the waist.

"My ladies have arrived," Daddy said. "Dinner will be ready soon."

Mama kissed Daddy on the cheek.

"Hey baby! I'm so glad you decided to cook. I've been running all day and my feet are killing me!"

"Y'all go get settled," Daddy said. "By the time you're done, everything will be ready."

Mama staggered to the master bedroom in exaggerated pain while Amber hurried upstairs to her room. Her phone buzzed as she reached the room; she smiled when she looked and saw Jasmine's name. She tossed her book bag on the floor then collapsed on her bed.

"Hey Queen!"
"Hey Queen!"
"What you doing?"

"Dinner."

"Cool. Hit me back when you're done. I have much dirt to share."

"Outstanding!"

At least some things didn't change. She and Jasmine were as tight as ever. They would get together on weekends, at least on the days Jasmine wasn't hanging out with her boyfriend, Carlos. She shook her head; never a million years would she have imagined Jasmine with him. But Carlos had 'blossomed;' he was no longer the gangly boy with the scary overbite and annoying voice. Time and the magic of dentistry had transformed him into a bae, as Jasmine called him. He still played video games too much in Amber's opinion, but when it came to boys, Amber's opinion never swayed Jasmine's decisions.

"Dinner's ready!" Daddy called out.

Amber hurried downstairs. She brushed by Daddy, took a plate from the cabinet, rushed to the pot of spaghetti and piled it on the plate. She took the lid off the sauce pot and drowned the spaghetti. When she turned around, Mama and Daddy stared at her, frowns on their faces.

"If anyone else saw you they would think you hadn't eaten in a month," Daddy said.

"But it's just us," Amber said with a sweet smile. Daddy smiled back, then went to make his own plate.

"She gets it from you," Mama said. "All that greediness."

"Guilty," Daddy replied as he filled his plate with noodles.

Amber was almost done by the time Mama and Daddy sat down.

"Slow down, child," Mama said. "That food ain't going nowhere."

"Got homework," Amber mumbled.

She finished off the spaghetti, chomped through her garlic bread, then went to the sink to wash her plate.

"I'll get that," Daddy said. "You go do your homework."

Amber dropped her plate on the counter, then scurried to the stairs.

"And don't be on the phone with Jasmine all night!" Mama called out.

"I won't!" Amber called back.

Amber closed her door, then grabbed her phone from her dresser. She jumped and landed on her bed, then rolled onto her back.

"Amber."

A warm sensation rushed through her and her eyes widened. She sat up, looking at her mirror. Her reflection shimmered then disappeared, replaced by the image of Grandma."

"Grandma!"

Amber jumped from the bed to the dresser, then grabbed the edges of the mirror.

"It's been so long! How are you?"

"I'm fine, baby," Grandma answered. "How are you? Are things going well with Bissau?"

"I'm good. Bissau is doing great. He gets on my nerves sometimes, though."

Grandma chuckled. "That's my Amber."

"I still don't understand why he's instructing me," she said.

"You're learning from each other," Grandma replied. "You are learning to use your powers and he is learning the ways of our world."

"He's doing a better job than I am."

"I'm sure you are both doing well. You are brilliant children."

Grandma's expression turned serious.

"Amber, I have something to tell you. Bagule is still alive."

Amber let go of the mirror, taking a few steps back. Her emotions roiled, churning from shock, relief and fear. She was relieved she had not killed someone, yet she knew if Bagule was alive, they were still in danger.

"Is he in the city?" she asked.

"We wish that were so," Grandma replied.

"Where is he?"

"We don't know. Baba Jakada senses his presence but cannot locate him. Aisha would know, but she has disappeared. You and Bissau must be diligent. He may have accepted his defeat, but that is unlikely."

Amber plopped down on her bed.

"Grandma, we have to tell Mama and Daddy," she said.

"We can't," Grandma replied. "Not yet. We can't tell anyone until we are ready."

"What if Bagule comes? What do I do then?"

"He won't come," Grandma said. "Bagule's goal is the city."

"But if he comes to the city, you may need my help," Amber said.

Grandma's silence was all Amber needed. She fell back on her bed.

"I can't handle this. I can't."

"You must," Grandma replied. "You have no choice."

Amber sat up, drained.

"I gotta go, Grandma," she said. "I have homework."

"I understand," Grandma said. "Do not worry. Everything will be fine."

"Bye, Grandma."

"Goodbye, Amber."

The mirror shimmered, then Grandma's image faded. Amber fell back on her bed again. The memories of her adventure with Grandma streamed through her head like a movie. Sometimes it didn't seem real; hopping from city to city, country to country; meeting amazing, magical people, and fighting for her life and the lives of others. It also placed a burden on her that she hoped she would never have to shoulder again. But here it was, right back in her face.

Her phone buzzed and she picked it up. It was Jasmine. Grandma's news sapped her energy; she didn't feel like texting. She set the phone back on the dresser. She looked at her desk, her textbook and computer waiting for her return. Amber sighed as she fell onto her back then rolled away so she couldn't see them. The phone buzzed again and she ignored it. Instead she grabbed her nightclothes, took a quick shower, then returned to the bed. She finally went to her phone; Bissau had texted as well. But Amber was done for the night. She put on her headphones, found a chill hip-hop video to listen to, then let the music lull her to sleep.

CHAPTER TWO

The man and woman strode the streets of Lagos with a confidence that did not match the simple clothing they wore. The man rubbed his beard as he walked, barely taking notice of the people and places surrounding him. When he did, he frowned in disappointment. The woman was just the opposite, her observant gaze capturing every face and evaluating them as either harmless or a threat. It had been this way ever since they were together. They depended on each other, and it was now more important than ever.

Bagule and Nieleni had adjusted to their new situation quickly. The first few days were a shock. Amber's blast did not kill them, but displaced them, dropping them into the middle of lifeless sand and dunes. The first weeks were perilous; they managed to survive by will and nyama alone. Eventually they found people and that's when their re-education began. The world outside of Marai had progressed far beyond the city in many ways, yet it was still the same in others. Their outfits did not attract as much attention as expected; many people still dressed in traditional clothing. They were destitute and for a time powerless. Bagule was distraught, thinking he had lost that which made him one of the most powerful people in Marai. But gradually his talents returned.

Nieleni was the first to adjust to their new circumstances. The poor of the outside world were not much different than those of Marai, except their plight was more desperate. It was she who acquired new clothes for them, a place to stay and eventually a means of income. Money was important in this world, much more than in theirs. It was also easy to gain, if a person was determined and ruthless.

"There," Nieleni pointed. Bagule frowned.

"Is this necessary?"

"It is the fastest way to get where we need to go."

Nieleni walked up to the machine then opened the door.

"You get in on the other side," she instructed.

Bagule walked around the car as if it was some strange beast. He grabbed the handle and pulled it; the door opened and he climbed inside. Nieleni smiled as she reached over him and pulled a strap across his chest.

"Seatbelt," she said. "It keeps you from being thrown outside if we have an accident."

Bagule looked concerned. "Are we going to have an accident?"

"Not if I can help it," Nieleni replied.

She buckled herself in, then pressed a button on the machine near the wheel. The car roared to life.

"Fascinating," Bagule said.

"Close your door," Nieleni instructed.

Bagule pulled his door shut.

"Are you sure this thing will get us to Songhai?"

"I'm sure. It's much faster than a camel and more comfortable, too."

"It's a machine," Bagule replied. "It may fail."

"It might, but if it does, we'll find other means."

"Such as a camel?"

Nieleni frowned. "If we must."

Bagule folded his arms. "When I claim Marai, these things will not be allowed in the city."

"As you wish." Nieleni pulled into the Lagos traffic. "But for now, we will use what we can."

Bagule frowned. Their time beyond the walls of the city had changed Nieleni, and not for the better. He would have to keep a closer eye on her.

Nieleni pressed another button and cool air filled the inside of the vehicle. Bagule smiled.

"Until then, I will enjoy the luxury."

They flowed with the congested traffic. Nieleni focused on the road with her natural intensity while Bagule observed the people. Outside of Marai he wasn't deterred by Jakada's restrictions. Although his power was drained after his confrontation with that insufferable girl Amber, he quickly recovered. It was then that he realized the barrier surrounding the city was not only a gate; it was also a cage that muted the powers of those trapped inside. Bagule never felt as powerful as he did at that moment, and his abilities increased daily. The people filling the streets did not interest him because of their garb and their manners; they interested him because of what hid among them.

"Stop the car," he said.

"I can't," Nieleni replied. "We're in the middle of traffic."

Bagule opened his door and began exiting the car.

"Bagule!" Nieleni slammed on the brakes, halting the car before Bagule's foot touched the pavement. He marched to the sidewalk, ignoring the curses and glares of the other drivers. He pushed into the crowd until he stood before a young man dressed in a smart atiku shirt and matching pants, dark shades hiding his eyes. The man stepped away from Bagule then took off his shades, his face reflecting his anger.

"What is wrong with you?" he said. "What do you want?"

Bagule grinned. "I know what you are."

The man's face calmed. "What do you mean, 'what I am?" You're crazy. Get away from me."

"You should be more respectful, djinn," Bagule said.

The man's face went slack.

"Come with me," Bagule said. "Or everyone else will know as well."

Bagule returned to the car and climbed back into the passenger seat. Nieleni glared at him.

"Why did you . . ."

The rear door to the car opened and the man Bagule accosted entered. Nieleni spun around.

"Who is this?"

"What is your name, djinn?" Bagule asked.

The man glared at Nieleni and Bagule.

"Oye," he said.

Bagule turned to look at the man. "What is your djinn name?"

"That is not your concern," he said. "What do you want?"

"Are you familiar with the city of Marai?"

Oye laughed. "Of course, I am. It was once a grand kingdom. It was destroyed hundreds of years ago. Why?"

"What if I was to tell you that Marai still exists, and that it has been hidden from the world since that time?"

Oye folded his arms. "That's impossible. Nyama that powerful doesn't exist anymore. If Marai was still here, we djinn would know."

It was Bagule's turn to laugh. "It seems the djinn are not as sensitive as they once were. Marai is alive and well. I can assure you of that."

"How?"

"Because we are from Marai," Bagule answered.

"Impossible!" the man said. "You're crazy, the both of you. I'm leaving."

The djinn reached for the door, then froze. He tried to grab the door handle but his hand would not move. He stared at Bagule.

"What are you?" he asked. "You are not a djinn and you are not a human."

"I am Bagule," he said. "As to what I am, that is of no concern for now. I need to find your city and speak to your ruler. I think I have something of interest."

Oye relaxed. "What?"

"I'll tell your ruler when I meet him."

"Her," Oye said "Mansa Nyima has no patience for humans. There is no way that will happen," Oye said. "Unless you bring something of value to her."

"And what would that be? Gold?"

Oye laughed. "Gold is like sand to her. There is only one item that would get you an audience with her."

"And what is that?"

"The Sword of Sonni Ali," Oye said.

Bagule rubbed his chin. "I thought so. Which is why we travel to Songhai."

Oye' eyes went wide and he laughed again.

"Maybe you are from Marai. There is no Songhai. The old kingdoms don't exist anymore."

Bagule grinned. "Are there people who still call themselves Songhai?"

"Yes," Oye answered.

"Then the kingdom lives. I suspect we will find that many of them still live in the region."

"Then I wish you luck," Oye said. "Now will you let me go?"

"You may leave," Bagule said.

The djinn slowly reached for the door handle. He grinned when he was able to touch it.

"I wish you luck, sorcerer of Marai," he said. "It's been a long time since a human attempted to visit the Mansa. I think she might be happy to see you after all, especially if you have the sword."

"I will have it," Bagule said. "You can be assured of it."

Oye opened the door and exited the car.

"Was it wise to let him go?" Nieleni asked.

"He will tell other djinn about us," Bagule said. "The word will eventually reach their Mansa."

"That may not be good for us."

"It will," Bagule replied. "Djinn are greedy creatures. They will search for the sword, and they will seek Marai. Both will serve my purpose. Our only challenge is to find the sword before they do."

"We will," Nieleni said.

"Of course," Bagule replied.

CHAPTER THREE

Alake ambled though the palace deep in thought. It had been over a year since she returned to Marai and she had yet to become settled. Her years in the world changed her in a way that kept her from fully embracing her former home, and the age reversal was jarring. Luckily her father was able to stop the process from reverting her to the age she was when she escaped the city. Alake had no desire to be an elder in a girl's body. That would make her transition even more awkward.

She ended her stroll outside Baba's room. She hesitated before entering, afraid of what he was working on. Amber had banished Bagule from Marai. Discovering he was still alive put everyone on guard once again. Bagule was a disturbance within the city. Outside the city he was a threat.

"Come in, Alake," Baba called out. She opened the door and entered. Baba stood before his mirror, passing his hands across the enchanted glass. He had gained weight, but he was still not up to full strength. Alake wasn't sure if he would ever regain his strength. He gave so much to Amber, and he still had to maintain the Veil protecting Marai from the rest of the world. She wished she could help him, but that was not her gift.

"How is it going?" she asked.

"Not well," Baba replied. "It's like looking for a particular grain of sand in the desert."

"Is there some way you could locate him using his nyama?"

Baba turned to face her, his serious expression letting her know he was about to share something she probably would not like.

"I could, but it would involve Amber and Bissau."

They had promised each other they would not involve the young ones unless it was absolutely necessary. Amber needed more training, and they had no idea how powerful Bagule would be without the restrictions of the Veil.

"Maybe she could help for a short time," Alake said. "She has the gift of reading. If she can find him, she can share with us his intentions."

Baba rubbed his chin. "The best way to accomplish that would be for me to locate him. That way Amber's contact with him would be brief."

Baba turned back to the mirror and continued scanning. Alake stood beside him, placing her hand on her back.

"You will find him," she said. "I know you will. Are you hungry?"

"Famished," Baba replied.

"I will make you something to eat."

"We have servants for that."

"Your daughter wishes to make you a meal. Do not interfere."

Baba chuckled. "Okay. Do what you wish."

Alake hurried from the Baba's room to the kitchen. The cooks were busy preparing meats and vegetables when she entered; they bowed in respect.

"How can we help you, mistress?" the head cook said.

"Do you have a goat butchered?" Alake asked.

"Yes, we do, mistress."

"Good."

Alake called out a list of ingredients for the staff to gather. She planned to prepare an old recipe of hers. Her only regret was that she didn't have shrimp or crab to make the meal complete. It was one of the foods she missed from the Low Country.

The servants brought the ingredients to her and Alake set about preparing the stew. She was dicing the onions when Baba's voice reached her.

"Alake! Alake! Come quickly!"

Alake dropped the knife and hurried to Baba's room. As she entered Baba met her with a wide grin.

"I found them!" he said. "Come see!"

Alake joined him in front of the mirror. A lone car traveled a dusty road that wound through the desert like an asphalt serpent. Baba maneuvered the image to reveal Nieleni's beautiful, yet serious face through the windshield. He moved the image again to reveal Bagule sitting on the passenger side, his eyes locked forward.

"We must know where he's going," Baba said. "Contact Amber."

Alake looked at her solar powered watch, one of the few luxuries she kept.

"It's late where she is," Alake said.

"Tell her to go to Bissau. His mirror is more powerful."

"It may be too late. She might not be able to leave the house without causing suspicion."

"We need her now, Alake," Baba said. "If we lose Bagule, it will be very difficult to find him again."

"I will try," Alake finally said.

She went to her room and stood before the mirror she used to communicate with Amber. After opening one of the leather pouches on the dresser, she withdrew a pinch of powder and blew it onto the mirror. Moments later the glass shimmered, revealing darkness.

"Amber?"

There was no reply.

"Amber?" Alake said louder.

"Wha . . ."

"Amber, it's Grandma. Wake up."

Amber appeared before the mirror. She was still dressed.

"Hey, Grandma," she said. "What's up?"

"Is it late?" Grandma asked.

"No," Amber replied. "I was just super-tired. I fell asleep doing my homework."

"Amber, I need you to go to Bissau's house now."

"I don't think I can do that, Grandma," Amber replied. "It's not late, but it's too late to go to a boy's house."

"Tell your mother you're going to Jasmine's house," Grandma replied.

Amber tilted her head as if in thought. "That might work. I'll try, but I can't promise anything."

"That's all I ask, Amber," Alake replied. "Be careful. I love you."

Amber smiled. "I will, Grandma. I love you too."

Alake broke contact. She sat before the mirror then massaged her forehead.

"I hope this is enough," she whispered. "I hope it all ends here."

CHAPTER FOUR

Amber's smile disappeared as soon as Grandma's image faded. What was she getting into now? She didn't have time for all this. Amber picked up her cell phone and texted Jasmine.

Hey Queen!
What's up, Queen?
I need a ride.
Where to?
I'll tell you when you get here.
Ooh, a mystery!
See you in a few.

She dressed then went downstairs to her parents' room.

"Mama? Daddy?"

The door opened and Mama stuck her head out, covered in her favorite night cap and matching house robe.

"What's wrong, Baby?" she asked.

"Nothing's wrong. I need to go to Jasmine's house for a minute."

"It's kinda late, isn't it?" Daddy called out. Amber peeked over Mama's shoulder to see Daddy sitting on their bed surfing the Net on his laptop.

"Yeah, but I'm working on some math and need some help. Jasmine's good at math."

Mama looked at her suspiciously. Daddy joined her at the door, then folded his arms.

"And how do you expect to get there?" he asked.

"Jasmine is picking me up."

Mama's eyes narrowed. "Don't y'all do that kind of stuff over the phone?"

"We usually do, but we need to be face to face for this stuff."

Mama's eyes narrowed as she leaned closer to Amber.

"I better not find out you're sneaking out to meet some boy," Mama whispered.

"I'm not," she said. "I promise."

Mama eyed her up and down.

"Okay, but don't stay over there too late. Homework or no, it's still a school night."

"Yes, ma'am," Amber said.

Amber walked back in the kitchen. How did Mama know these things? She was going to see a boy, but not for the reasons Mama assumed. Maybe it was because she did the same thing when she was her age. The thought made her laugh. Grandma did say Mama was 'fast' when she was younger.

Her phone buzzed.

Almost there, Queen.

Amber grabbed cookies from the counter and poured a glass of milk. She finished the last cookie when her phone buzzed again.

I'm here.

"I'll be back in a few," Amber called out as she jogged to the front door.

"Alright, Baby!" Mama shouted back. "Be safe."

Amber left through the front door and continued to jog to Jasmine's car. Jasmine got her driver's license two months ago and her parents gave her a used Honda Accord as a celebration gift. Amber admired her. Amber was terrified of driving. Mama and Daddy had attempted to teach her a number of times, but she always froze when she sat behind the wheel.

Amber walked around the car, then jumped into the passenger seat. Jasmine greeted her with a grin.

"So, where we going?"

"I need you to take me to Bissau's house.

Jasmine's eyes went wide.

"What! Girl . . ."

Amber rolled her eyes. "It's not what you think."

"How you do know what I'm thinking?"

"Because it's always what you're thinking," Amber replied. "I need him to help me with some homework. I knew Mama and Daddy wouldn't let me go if she knew it was him and there was no way they'd let him come to our house."

"So, I'm an accessory to a conspiracy?"

Amber laughed. "You're always so dramatic. Just take me the boy's house."

"What's his address?"

Amber texted the address to Jasmine and she looked it up on the GPS.

"Let's ride!" she said.

Amber and Jasmine arrived at Bissau's apartment complex five minutes later. Jasmine pulled up to the talk box and Amber punched in the code.

"You know his security code?" Jasmine asked.

"Yep. We're friends."

"Yeah, right."

Amber glared at Jasmine. "Shut it."

Bissau's voice broke their back and forth.

"Yes? Who is it?"

"Hi Bissau. It's Amber. Buzz me in."

"Amber? What are you doing here? Are you with your parents?"

"Just buzz me in, okay? Grandma contacted me."

The gate buzzed, then opened. Amber climbed back into the car.

"We're looking for Building 214."

"Gotcha."

Amber marveled at the apartment complex while Jasmine cruised through. How could Bissau afford this? She knew he was alone, so she had no idea how he managed to pay rent. And how did he get away with school without parents? Every time she asked him, he never answered. One day, she was going to corner him and find out.

"Here we are," Jasmine said. She parked in front of the building.

"I'll be back," Amber said.

"Oh no, sister! You're not leaving me out here!"

"It's just going to be a minute!"

Jasmine's expression told Amber everything she needed to know.

"Okay, but you have to promise me you won't tell anybody about anything you see or hear. Okay?"

Jasmine's eyebrows rose. "What exactly am I going to see or hear?"

"Promise me, Jasmine!"

Jasmine rolled her eyes. "I promise."

Amber climbed out of the car. "Come on."

They walked up the stairs to the second floor. Amber knocked. She heard the door unlock, then it creaked open. Bissau peeked outside.

"It is you!" he said.

"Who else would it be? Let us in."

"Us?"

"Jasmine's with me."

"She shouldn't be."

Amber sighed. "I had no choice. She's my ride and she wouldn't stay in the car."

Bissau opened the door, then stepped aside. Amber walked in and was stunned. She expected a sparse interior, but the apartment was immaculate.

"Bissau, how did you do this?"

"Do not ask," he said. "Come, let's contact Alake."

Jasmine cleared her throat. Bissau looked at her and forced a smile.

"Hello Jasmine. Please make yourself comfortable. We'll only be a few minutes."

Jasmine nodded as she went directly to the refrigerator.

"Follow me, Amber."

Amber trailed Bissau to his bedroom. Like the family room, his room was perfect. He opened the top drawer of his dresser and took out a small pouch. He took a pinch of powder then blew it into the mirror. The mirror wavered, then Grandma's image appeared.

"Good, you are together," she said.

"Hello Alake," Bissau said. "How may I serve you?"

"As you know, Bissau is outside the city. Jakada has finally found him. He is on a road in a desert. That is all we know."

"What can we do?" Amber said.

"Jakada wishes to know his destination and his intentions. He wants you to connect to him so you can find out."

Amber stepped away from the mirror.

"I'm not sure about that," she said. "What if he discovers it's us?"

"It's a chance we have to take."

Amber folded her arms, fighting the fear that was rising into her throat.

"But what if he finds out it's me? He tried to kill me."

Grandma closed her eyes for a moment. She opened them.

"Amber, I understand how you feel."

"No, Grandma. I don't think you do."

Grandma was silent for a long moment.

"It's up to you, Amber," she finally said. "I'm sure Baba can find him by other means, but if you help us it would save so much time."

Amber felt Bissau's hand on her shoulder.

"Amber," he said. "You must do this. Bagule is a dangerous man, especially now that he is beyond the walls of Marai."

"Bissau, I don't know if . . ."

A knock on the door interrupted Amber's words.

"Hey, what's going on in there?" Jasmine said. "Whatever it is, I hope you're done soon. I got to get home!"

Amber rolled her eyes.

"A few more minutes, Jazz!" Amber shouted.

"Your friend is annoying," Bissau said.

"My friend is worried about me," Amber replied. "As a good friend should be. We have been in here for a while."

"What are you going to do?" Bissau asked.

Amber faced the mirror. She took a deep breath, then extended her hands toward the surface. She had no idea what to do, and no one seemed to know how to help her. She shrugged.

"Show me Bagule," she said.

Amber's hands tingled as she uttered the last word. Her palms warmed, and a pinkish glow surrounded her fingers for a brief moment before drifting into the mirror. The reflective surface glittered then swirled like water descending into a drain. Amber felt dizzy, then weightless. Tearing her gaze from the mirror, she glanced down at her feet to make sure they were still touching the floor. They weren't.

"What is happening?" she said, her voice full of worry.

"Concentrate," Bissau said.

"Okay, that's it!"

Bissau's door banged then flew open. Jasmine glared at Amber and Bissau, her hands balled into fists.

"What are you doing to my . . . oh my goodness! Amber, you're floating!"

Amber dropped to the floor. She looked at Jasmine's shocked face.

"Uh, Jasmine . . . let me explain . . ."

Jasmine raised her hands. "I'm just going to go back to the den and sit down. Y'all let me know when y'all are done. Yeah, that's what I'm going to do."

She backed away for a moment, then turned and ran. Amber started to follow, but Bissau grabbed her wrist.

"Amber, you must finish what you started," he said.

"But Jasmine saw us!" Amber blurted.

"Yes, she did. We'll have to explain it to her later. But right now, you have to locate Bagule."

Amber turned back to the mirror. She needed to finish this and get to Jasmine. This could get out of hand quickly. She opened her hands and the mirror swirled again. An image of a road surrounded by desert appeared, a thin line winding between massive dunes. Amber concentrated and the road widened. A car traveled the road, dodging potholes. Amber's stomach ached as she watched Bagule sitting in the passenger seat, his demeanor unnervingly calm. Nieleni drove, her eyes focused on the road ahead of them.

"I found them," she said. "Can I go now?"

"Not yet," Grandma replied. "We still don't know where they are."

Amber felt something enter her head.

"What's happening, Grandma?" she asked, her voice wavering.

"It's me," she said. "Just be still for a few moments."

Amber did as Grandma told, Bagule and Nieleni still in her view. The pair was silent, the miles of featureless road speeding by.

"There," Grandma finally said. "I know where they are and I have an idea where they are heading. You can come back now."

"Thank goodness!" Amber exclaimed.

Amber was about to pull away from the image when something grabbed her.

"What is . . ."

Bagule's head turned toward her. He stared directly into her eyes then smiled.

"Hello, Amber."

"What?!"

Amber tried to pull away, but Bagule held onto her.

"As you can see, I am still alive," he said. "I would love to talk, but we are quite busy. We will see each other again. Soon."

Bagule waved his hand and Amber was thrown back. Bissau caught her before she hit the floor.

"Amber! What happened?"

Amber's head ached. Bissau eased her to the floor as she rubbed her forehead.

"Bagule," she said. "He saw me."

Bissau sat beside her then placed his arm around her shoulder.

"What do you mean he saw you?"

Bissau's question angered her. She pushed his arm from her shoulder then stood, her fingers balled into fists. Her necklaced warmed.

"He saw me! I knew I shouldn't have done this! I'm going home."

She started for the door. Bissau grabbed at her arm and before she could think, she spun and pushed him, the necklace hot on her neck. Bissau flew across the room, then slammed against the wall.

"Oh my God," Amber exclaimed as she hurried to Bissau. "I'm sorry! I'm so sorry!"

Bissau waved her away. When he looked up at her, his eyes were narrowed. For the first time she could remember, Bissau was angry at her.

"Go," he said. "Just go."

"Bissau, I didn't . . ."

"Go, Amber. Please."

Amber rushed from the room. Jasmine was on her feet, concern on her face.

"Amber, what happened? It sounded like y'all were fighting."

"We weren't," Amber said. "Let's go."

Amber walked out of the house to the car, Jasmine on her heels. They left Bissau's apartment quickly and climbed into Jasmine's car. They were almost back to Amber's house before Jasmine spoke.

"So, are we going to talk about it?"

Amber looked at her friend. "Talk about what?"

"About what I saw. About you hovering over the ground and looking into a mirror that wasn't a mirror."

"No," Amber replied.

Jasmine jerked the steering wheel to the right and guided the car off the road into a fast-food restaurant parking lot. She shut off the engine.

"Yes, we are," she said.

"Look, Jasmine, I know things looked crazy, but you wouldn't believe me if I tried."

"I saw you floating, Amber. Floating! At this point, I'm open to believe just about anything."

Amber sighed. Once she told Jasmine, she would be a part of whatever was going on, and she didn't want that to happen.

"I don't want to get you involved," she said.

"If you didn't want that, you wouldn't have asked me to take you to Bissau's house."

"You weren't supposed to see anything."

Jasmine touched her shoulder.

"Look, girl, I'm your friend. Your best friend. You know I'm down with you no matter what, right?"

Amber looked into Jasmine's eyes and saw the sincerity in her words. She didn't need her abilities to tell her so, but it was nice to have them to confirm what she always knew. She took a deep breath.

"Remember that trip I took to Europe and Africa with my Grandma?"

"You mean the one where you were in the room with a boy?"

Amber rolled her eyes. "Yeah, that one. Well, it wasn't exactly a vacation. Grandma took me to a city called Marai so I could pick their next king."

Jasmine eyes widened. "What the what?"

Amber told Jasmine everything. When she was done, Jasmine sat there silent for a few minutes before saying anything.

"You know, under any other circumstances, I would jump out this car and run all the way home screaming, but I saw you float. So I figure if you can do that, everything else must be true."

"Please don't tell anyone," Amber pleaded.

"You ain't got to worry about that," Jasmine said. "The last thing I need is my parents thinking I'm crazy. They're still trying to figure out why I'm dating Carlos."

"I am, too," Amber said.

"Shut it," Jasmine snapped. "So, what does Bissau have to do with all this?"

"He's the protégé of my great-grandfather. He's supposed to be helping me develop my talents, but he's not that great at it."

"Is he the boy from the room?" Jasmine asked.

"Yes."

"He's hot," Jasmine said with a mischievous smile.

"Not you, too," Amber said.

"I call it like I see it," Jasmine said. "Are y'all dating?"

"No!" Amber exclaimed. "He's just my guide. Once I've learned all what I need to know, he'll return to Marai."

"And what are you learning to do?" Jasmine asked.

"Control my abilities," she answered.

"And when you do?"

Amber opened her mouth then shut it.

"I . . . I honestly don't know."

"Seems to me that you should have asked before you signed up for all this."

Jasmine started the car, then steered it back to the parking lot entrance. After a quick check, she merged into traffic. Amber looked out the passenger window, ruminating on Jasmine's question. Why was she doing all this? Her duty had been to choose the next ruler of Marai and she'd done it. Well, she'd at least tried to. The other abilities she possessed were unusual to Grandma and great-grandfather as well.

"We're here."

Amber had been so distracted that she didn't notice when they arrived at her house. She unbuckled her seat belt, then leaned over to hug her friend.

"Thank you so much, Queen," she said.

"Don't mention it, Queen," Jasmine replied.

Amber exited the car, then hurried up the driveway.

"Hey!"

Amber turned to Jasmine.

"You're going to be okay, aren't you?" Jasmine asked.

"I'll be okay," Amber said. "It's an ability, not an illness."

"Yeah, but still, you be careful. I love you, Queen."

"I love you, too, Queen."

Jasmine backed out of the driveway, then drove away. Amber let herself into the house, shutting off the alarm and the outdoor floodlights. When she turned on the family room lights, she saw Daddy sitting on the couch.

"Did you get all your studying done?" he asked.

"Yeah," Amber said. She went to the refrigerator and took out a bottled water. Amber twisted off the cap as she ambled into the family room, then sat by Daddy.

"You waited up for me?" she said as innocent as she could.

"Of course, I did," he replied. "It's not like you to go out this time of night on a weekday."

"Had some serious work to do," Amber said. "And it was good to see Jasmine."

"How're her parents?" Daddy asked.

Amber shrugged. "I don't know. I didn't ask."

"That's okay. I'll give her dad a call tomorrow."

Daddy scooted closer to her, then put his arm around her.

"Is everything okay?"

Amber snuggled against him, then closed her eyes. For a brief moment, she wanted to tell him everything. She wanted to tell him about Grandma, about Great-Granddaddy, about Marai, about Bissau, but most of all, she wanted to tell him about Bagule. A part of her wanted him to protect her, but she knew he couldn't."

"Everything's fine," she answered.

"I know changing schools wasn't easy," he said. "Leaving your old friends is tough. But believe me when I say it's for the best. It's hard to see now, but everything will become clearer later. That's how life works."

"I understand," she said.

Amber finished her water. She threw the bottle in the garbage, then shuffled over to daddy and kissed his cheek.

"I love you, Daddy."

Daddy hugged her tight.

"I love you too, Baby. See you in the morning."

Amber hurried upstairs to her bedroom. She showered, put on her nightclothes then fell into the bed exhausted and exasperated. She looked at the mirror and was tempted to contact grandma, but she had enough for the night. Instead she put in her ear pods, pulled up her smooth jazz playlist then tried to sleep. After a fitful few minutes, she did.

CHAPTER FIVE

Bissau watched Jasmine and Amber drive away from his bedroom window. He waited until the car passed through the security gate and was out of sight before trudging to his bed and sitting down hard. He sighed, then opened his dresser drawer and took out the pouch where he kept his powder. Bissau took a pinch from the pouch, placed it in his left hand, then blew it gently into the mirror. Seconds later, the mirror shimmered before revealing the innards of Master Jakada's bedchamber. The elderly man sat on his gilded stool, fully dressed as if he expected Bissau to contact him. Bissau smiled. Knowing Master Jakada, he probably did.

"Bissau," he said. "What troubles you?"

"Master, I am concerned," Bissau said. "You sent me here to watch over Amber and guide her as she learns of her abilities. I believe I am failing her."

Master Jakada's eyebrows lifted. "Why do you think so?"

"You saw her today," he said. "She was reluctant to help you, and when she became angry, she attacked me. Her power is much greater than any of us realize, and I am not sure I can be of any help."

"What do you suggest, Bissau?" Master Jakada asked.

"You are asking me, Master?"

Jakada nodded. "You have spent more time with her than I have. Your opinion has value."

"I believe we should return to Marai," he said. "I think that you and Alake would be better for her than I alone."

"Do you wish this for Amber, or do you wish this for yourself?"

Bissau began to speak, then hesitated. He could not lie to Master Jakada.

"I believe it is best for both of us."

Master Jakada stood, then paced.

"Bissau, in all my years of training young people, I have never met anyone more talented than you," he said. "You contain an amazing combination of strength, intelligence, and wisdom far beyond anyone your age and most adults. The only young person rivaling your talents is Amber. That is why I gave you this task."

"But Master, you saw what happened today. She doesn't listen to me. She doesn't do as I ask!"

"She's not supposed to," Master Jakada said. "You are not her teacher, nor are you her mentor. You are her companion. She has strengths that you do not possess, and you have abilities she lacks. Together you are powerful, because you are equal."

Bissau shook his head. "I don't understand. You paired us so we can learn from each other?"

"Yes," Master Jakada confirmed. "Amber should not only listen to you; you should listen to her."

Bissau was quiet for a moment as he processed Master Jakada's words.

"What can Amber teach me?"

"That, I cannot reveal," Master Jakada said. "Only time and experience can show you."

"I understand," Bissau said.

"There is something else I must share with you," Master Jakada said.

"I didn't expect Bagule to survive Amber's outburst. Now that he is beyond the barrier, his powers will fully manifest. He was a problem within the city; outside he is a more dangerous threat. I know where he is going, and I know what he is seeking."

"What is it?" Bissau said.

"Many centuries ago, the Maraibu were allied with many kingdoms, some of this world, others not. One of those kingdoms was the realm of the djinn."

Bissau had heard of the djinn, but he had never encountered them.

"I believe Bagule is seeking them out," Master Jakada continued.

"Why?" Bissau asked.

"Bagule may be thinking of forming an alliance with them against Marai."

"Is that possible?"

"I want to say no, but I can't rule it out."

"What makes the djinn so special?"

Master Jakada returned to his stool and sat.

"The djinn are special beings. As you know, our barrier keeps the Maraibu in and others out. However, our barrier does not work against djinn. They can come and go as they please."

"So, if Bagule finds the djinn and forms an alliance with them, they can attack Marai through the Veil!"

"Yes," Master Jakada said.

Bissau jumped to his feet. "Then we must stop him!"

"Yes, we must, but not by pursuing him."

"Then how?"

The djinn will not accept any alliance with humans. They see us as beneath them. Only one person has ever controlled the djinn. It was Sonni Ali, the first emperor of Songhai. Ali possessed a sword of such power that it helped him forge his empire and control the djinn. If somehow Bagule knows this, he is probably seeking the sword. It makes sense that he would go to Djenne, for if any knowledge of its whereabout exists, it would be in that sacred city."

"Then we must go to Djenne to stop him!" Bissau said.

"That is not so easy," Master Jakada replied.

"Then what must we do?" Bissau asked.

"I need time to think," Jakada replied. "When I have a solution, I will contact you. Until then, continue to guide Amber. Work hard to get her to listen to you. In turn, you must listen to her."

"I will, Master," Bissau said.

"Goodbye for now, Apprentice," Master Jakada said.

Bissau bowed. "Goodbye, Master."

Jakada's image faded. Bissau stood, rubbing his shoulder where he struck the wall. He would take a warm shower and go to bed. In the morning he would begin his duty again. But now, he would be the student as well.

CHAPTER SIX

Bagule smiled as Amber's image faded. Nieleni looked back at him with concern.

"They know," she said. "We must prepare."

"We'll do nothing different," Bagule replied. "We continue with our plan. Jakada is no threat outside of Marai."

"I'm not worried about Jakada," Nieleni said. "I'm worried about Amber. If they send the girl after us before we contact the djinn, she may thwart our plans."

"Amber will not come for us," Bagule said. "She is afraid."

"How do you know?"

"I sensed it," Bagule said. "She was afraid before, and she is more fearful now. What she did to us was not planned or expected. She reacted instinctively."

Bagule hesitated before continuing. He was not one to readily admit his mistakes.

"I underestimated her," he finally said. "I won't do it again."

"Let's hope not," Nieleni said. "Our success depends on your good judgment."

Bagule was taken aback by Nieleni's words. Never before had she doubted him. His failure to protect them must have shaken her.

"You won't have to worry about anything happening like that again," he said. "I rarely make mistakes, and I only make them once."

Nieleni cut her eyes at Bagule. "Let's hope so."

They continued their journey, stopping to refuel and eat. After a number of border crossings, they finally arrived in the country now known as Mali. Although it had been centuries since he last traveled to the Sahel, enough remained to spark a bit of nostalgia inside him. He recalled the massive caravans that traveled from Marai to the empire, camels laden with sorghum, dates, fabrics and magical talisman. Many others would come to study in the numerous universities with learned imams, taking the knowledge back to the city. It was a prosperous time cut short by Jakada and his cursed barrier. But that was about to change.

Bagule's full memory returned when they finally reached Djenne. The old mud mosques still stood, as did many of the stone buildings. Camel and donkey traffic had been mostly replaced by modern cars and trucks, although a few people still used traditional transportation. The people wore a mix of modern and traditional clothing.

"Let's park," Bagule said.

Nieleni found an open space then parked the car. Bagule climbed out then looked about. A man wearing a uniform caught his attention; he approached the man with a disarming smile.

"As Salam u Alaikum," he said.

The man smiled. "Wa Alaikum Salaam. How can I help you?"

"My name is Bagule. It has been a long time since I've visited Djenne. Tell me, does the Bambari library still exist?"

The man laughed. "It has been a long time since you've been here. Centuries, it seems."

Both men laughed.

"Good thing I'm a student of history, or I wouldn't have an answer for you. The Bambari library is now part of the National Museum. It's only a few blocks from here."

The man gave Bagule the directions. He returned to the car where Nieleni waited.

"The library is straight ahead," he said.

Nieleni started the car, then drove to their destination. The National Museum rested on the corner of the main road and a lesser street. It was built in the fashion of the mud mosques, except the mud had been replaced with stucco. The building seemed weathered, but was still in decent shape. Nieleni parked and they proceeded to the entrance. They were about to go inside when Bagule stopped.

"A djinn resides here," he said.

"Is that a problem?" Nieleni asked.

"It could be," Bagule said. "There's only one way to find out."

He entered the building, Nieleni close behind and on guard. A wave of nostalgia hit Bagule as he gazed upon the various items on display. They reminded him of an earlier time when the kingdoms of the Sahel were the wealthiest and most powerful kingdoms in the world. Marai was among them and would still be great if not for Jakada's stupid ideas.

"Can I help you?"

Bagule and Nieleni's heads turned toward the sound. A tall woman emerged from the darkness. Her bright clothes accented her dark skin and vibrant jewelry. The smile on her face vanished as she came closer. There was poison in her voice when she spoke.

"What do you want, Sorcerer?"

Bagule smiled. "You are more perceptive than your kin in Lagos."

The woman sucked her teeth. "You must be talking about Oye. He is a fool."

"I would think djinn would be more respectful of each other."

"We are no different from humans in that regard."

The woman placed her hands on her hips.

"I ask you again, what do you want, Sorcerer?"

"I wish to meet with the Djinn Mansa," Bagule said.

The woman threw back her head in laughter.

"Go away, Sorcerer. I have no time for your games."

Nieleni stepped forward, her hand rising to guard position.

"Do not speak to him like that!" she said.

The djinn reached out with her left hand and Nieleni clutched her throat, her eyes wide. The djinn lifted her arm and Nieleni rose from the ground.

"Enough!" Bagule said.

He waved his hand and Nieleni fell. She collapsed to her knees then rubbed her throat. The djinn's eyebrows rose.

"You have some skill," she said. "I should test you."

"Do you think that wise?" Bagule replied.

The djinn tapped her finger on her chin, as if considering. Bagule glared defiantly while secretly hoping the djinn would not challenge him. It had taken him all his strength to break her grip on Nieleni. He would fail any contest she threw his way.

"Your bravery impresses me," she said. "I will let you live, although if you seek the Mansa, your reprieve will be short."

"Oye told me that I can gain an audience with her if I bring her the Sword of Sonni Ali. I came here for your help to find it."

"I cannot help you," the djinn said.

"But this was once his homeland, wasn't it?"

The djinn shrugged. "Rivers once flowed through the grasslands of this land. Now it is desert. There is always a once. Things change."

"So, you're saying the Sword is no longer in Djenne?"

"It may be, it may not be," the djinn answered. "If any djinn knew where it was, they haven't looked. That thing was a scourge to our kind. It is said that Askia Muhammad claimed it from Sonni Ali's son and destroyed it. If so, good riddance. The djinn served one human; we were not about to serve two."

"How would I find it?"

"You think I would tell you?"

Bagule smiled. "You will not help me find it, but you won't try to stop me, will you?"

The djinn smiled. "No. I won't. I have better things to do with my time."

"Good. I will be sure to let the Mansa know of your assistance."

The djinn turned and walked away.

"Feel free to use the services of the museum," she called out.

Bagule continued to stare at the djinn until she disappeared. He hurried to Nieleni.

"Are you okay?'

Nieleni massaged her neck. "I will be. Thank you for saving me. I know it took a great amount of *nyama* to do so."

"You are worth every bit of it," he replied. They smiled at each other, the first time they'd acknowledged their feelings for each other in a long time.

"Come," he said. "Let's find a place to stay and get something to eat. I don't think the sword is here, but I think we'll find out where it is."

CHAPTER SEVEN

Amber woke the next morning, tossing her bedsheet aside and beating her mattress with her fists. She didn't want to go to school; she didn't want to go to life. She wanted to roll back time and erase yesterday. Instead she sighed and climbed out of bed to begin her morning ritual.

After washing up and dressing she trudged downstairs for breakfast. Daddy was hovering over the stove as always, fixing a hot breakfast. Mama sat at the kitchen dinette, flipping through her phone. She looked up, a big smile gracing her face.

"Good morning, Baby!" she chirped.

Amber plopped into her chair. "I'm not a baby. Stop calling me that." Amber was not in the mood for her cheerfulness.

Mama's smile faded. "Uh oh. Someone's in a bad mood. Talk to your daughter, Husband."

Daddy shook his head. "Not this morning."

Daddy made their plates. There were grits, scrambled eggs and link sausages, Amber's favorite breakfast. But even looking at the morning feast didn't pull her out of her mood. She ate in silence. When she was done, she washed her plate and left the kitchen.

"I'll be in my room when you're ready, Mom," she said.

"She called me Mom," her mother said. "She must really be pissed off."

Amber ignored Mama's jab and returned to her room. She fell back on her bed, then turned on some music. She felt bad;

bad about discovering Bagule, bad about exposing Jasmine to her secret, but most of all she felt bad about hurting Bissau. He was right, she needed to learn how to control her powers, at least what she knew about them. She touched her necklace. Maybe she shouldn't wear it unless she was in training. Grandma told her to never take it off, but it seemed to cause more trouble then she needed. She was reaching for the clasp when Mama's shrill voice invaded her room.

"Let's go, Baby Girl!" she shouted.

Mama calling her baby girl made her grin.

"You're so petty," she whispered as she left her room.

Mama met her at the garage door and they loaded into the car and headed to school. Thankfully, Mama was on the phone the entire ride, setting up real estate appointments. When they reached school, Amber managed to escape the car without the customary kiss on the cheek. She was beginning to be proud of herself when she saw Bissau waiting for her.

"Oh no," she whispered. She forced a smile to her face.

"Hi, Bissau," she said.

"Hello, Amber," he replied. "Can I talk to you for a minute?"

"I'm sorry about last night," she blurted. "You told me I should work on my control and you were right. I didn't mean to hurt you."

Bissau smiled. "It's okay, Amber. I need to apologize, too. I have misinterpreted my duties when it comes to you. I had a long talk with Master Jakada last night and he helped me understand the error of my ways."

Amber was confused.

"What are you talking about?"

Bissau placed his hand on her shoulder.

"I am not your teacher," he said. "The fact is that we are both students. If you need my help, ask me and I will do my best. But I ask that you do the same for me."

"Uh . . . okay," Amber replied.

The first bell rang. Bissau gestured toward the school entrance.

"Come on. I'll walk you to your homeroom class."

"That'll be great," Amber replied.

"Hold up, Amber girl!"

Amber closed her eyes in annoyance. Bissau turned to the direction of the voice and frowned.

"It's your friend, Britani," he said.

"Run for your life," Amber replied.

Bissau chuckled. "Too late."

Britani trotted over to join them. She worked her way between them then grinned at Bissau.

"Hey Bissau," she said. "You look good today."

Amber shook her head, attempting to stop Bissau from saying what she knew he was going to say.

"Hello, Britani. You look good as well."

Amber rolled her eyes as Britani lit up like sunshine.

"You think so? Thank you!"

They walked together until Amber reached her homeroom class. The rest of the day was a mundane blur. It was spring, and most of her teachers were reviewing the year's work in preparation for the upcoming finals. Amber went through the motions; she was ready for the finals, ready to get them over with and ready for the summer to begin. She was relieved to get the day over with and looked forward to soccer practice.

She made a quick change into her practice gear, then headed for the field. Britani met her halfway.

"Bissau is so sweet!" she said. "You sure you two ain't a thing?"

"We're not," Amber said. "Go for it."

"What you think I'm doing?" Britani said. "He keeps being polite. I'm waiting for him not to be."

"Bissau is kind of naïve when it comes to stuff like that," Amber said. "You'll have to be direct with him."

"Direct, how?"

"Kiss him," Amber said.

Britani's eyes went wide. "For real? You mean just kiss him for no reason?"

"You have a reason," Amber said. "Just kiss him and get it over with."

"But what if he doesn't like it?"

"Then you'll know, and he'll know and you both can stop wasting each other's time."

"But what if he does?"

Amber stopped. What if he did? How would that affect his relationship with her? And why was she even thinking about that?

Amber shrugged. "Then you'll have a boyfriend."

Britani smiled so hard Amber expected a tooth to pop out of her mouth.

"That would be perfect!"

Amber frowned. "Great. Now let's talk about something else."

Apparently, there was nothing else Britani wanted to talk about. Amber was relieved when Coach Sandalwood blew the whistle for practice to begin. The girls gathered around for their assignments for the day.

"Okay ladies, we're only a week away from the beginning of the season. We did a good job last year, but the other teams did better. Not this year. I've made some changes to the line-up that should guarantee a playoff spot."

The coach read off the list. Amber's mind was drifting to the night before until she heard her name.

"Amber, you'll be switching to defense."

Amber jerked up her head.

"What?"

Coach Sandalwood frowned.

"I said you'll play defense this year. You did such a great job during practice, I think you'll be a major asset."

"No!" Amber blurted.

Coach Sandalwood's hands dropped to her hips.

"What did you say?"

Amber hesitated. Whatever words came out of her mouth next would make the difference between her playing or sitting the bench. At the same time, a resolve grew, emboldened by her warming necklace.

"No," she said again. "I'm not playing defense."

The coach glared at her. "You play the position you're assigned."

"No," Amber said one more time. "I came to this stupid school because my parents made me. They said coming here would be better for me academically and athletically. And now you're moving me to a position that I'm not good at. I'm a forward. That's what I do. I quit."

Amber spun, then stomped away.

"Amber! Amber Robinson! You get back here right now!"

Amber continued to walk away. When she reached the locker room, she changed back into her school clothes, then hurried away. She texted her Mama.

Hey Mama! Practice ended early. Can you pick me up?
I'll be right there, Baby Girl.

Amber was striding to the parking lot when she heard Britani call her name. She turned to see her friend running toward her.

"Amber, wait!"

Amber kept walking until she reached the bench near bus stop, then sat down. Britani sat beside her.

"Wow, girl! You just quitting like that?"

"I don't feel like talking right now," Amber said.

"You can't just quit!"

"I just did."

"What are your parents gonna say?"

"I don't know, and I don't care."

Britani put her arm around Amber and her necklace flared. Britani's arm flew off her shoulder.

"Ow!"

Amber jumped up, her eyes wide.

"What you do that for?" Britani said. "I didn't do nothing to you!"

Amber felt a bit of relief. Britani thought she pushed her arm away. She didn't see what really happened. Amber balled her fists, fighting down her emotions. She wasn't going to hurt Britani like she hurt Bissau.

"I'm sorry," she said between clenched teeth. "I didn't mean it."

Britani rubbed her shoulder and smiled.

"It's good. Come on back to practice."

Amber's eyes narrowed. "Did Coach send you?"

"No. I came on my own. You're my girl. Playing defense ain't so bad. Besides, you're good at it."

Amber sat down. "That's not why she put me there. You know why she did it."

Britani sat beside her. "Yeah, I know. It's not right."

"Tell me about it."

They heard a car horn blow. Amber looked up to see Mama pulling into the parking lot.

"I gotta go," she said.

"What are you going to tell your parents?"

"I'm going to tell them the truth," Amer said. "They'll either get mad at me or they'll understand. Either way, I'm not on the team anymore."

Britani hugged her.

"Good luck, Sister. No matter what you think, I hope you come back."

She trotted back to the practice field. Amber took a deep breath as Mama pulled up. She opened the door, then climbed inside. Mama looked at her with a skeptical expression.

"Okay, Amby," she said. "What's really going on? I know for a fact Coach Sandalwood didn't end practice early. That woman would keep y'all until midnight if she could."

"I quit the team," Amber said.

"You what?"

"I quit the team," Amber repeated. "Coach wants me to play defense this year. I'm not going to."

"Why does she want you to play defense? You're a forward. You've always been a forward."

"Because she wants to give more shine to her pet player," Amber said.

"Oh no she doesn't!"

Mama parked the car and took off her seatbelt.

"Me and this Coach Sandalwood are about to have a talk."

"No Mama," Amber pleaded. "I'm embarrassed enough. Let's just go home. Please?"

Mama looked at Amber and her expression softened.

"Okay, Baby. We'll go home. But believe me when I say this is not over."

Mama buckled up and they drove away.

"How long has this been going on?" Mama asked.

"I can't say," Amber replied. "At first, I thought she was just making everyone switch positions during practice so we could feel what everyone did on the team. But then, she kept playing me on defense and I knew something was wrong."

"Who is this other girl?"

"It's not her fault," Amber said.

"I didn't ask you that," Mama replied. "Who is she?"

"Cynthia Radcliff," Amber answered. She knew better than to challenge Mama when she was in this mood.

"Her name doesn't sound familiar," Mama mused. "Probably the daughter of some big donor. I remember when I was a cheerleader in high school. There was this girl named Teresa Hill. Girl couldn't do a cartwheel, but she made the squad because her mother and father were well-known in town and they wanted to see their daughter cheering the team on. It wasn't fair then, and it's not fair now."

"I don't want to talk about it," Amber said. "I just want to go home."

"Okay, Baby," Mama said. "We'll swing by Mai's for dinner." The mention of her favorite Vietnamese restaurant brightened her mood a bit.

"That sounds great," Amber said. "Thanks, Mama."

Mama called in the order, then detoured into town to pick up their meal. Daddy's car was in the garage when they pulled in; apparently, he was home early as well. When they walked in, they caught him pulling pots out of the cabinet.

"Put that stuff away," Mama said. "I brought dinner."

"Daddy turned to them and smiled. "I see. I smell com!"

His eyes fell on Amber and she turned away.

"Uh oh," he said. "What's wrong?"

Amber was about to tell Daddy, but Mama spoke first.

"Amber quit the soccer team," she said.

Daddy's eyes went wide. "She what?"

"I quit the team," Amber said.

Amber braced herself for a lecture. Instead, Daddy took her hand and led her to the kitchen table.

"Sit down and tell me what happened," he said.

Amber sat. She held onto Daddy's hand as she answered.

"Coach Sandalwood moved me to defense," she said.

"That's not your position," Daddy said. "That's not why you transferred. Why did she do that?"

"Because she wanted to give the position to some girl named Cynthia Radcliff!" Mama said.

Daddy closed his eyes as a knowing smile came to his face.

"I've heard of the Radcliffs. Very prominent family; big school donors. Cynthia is probably their granddaughter. Amber, is she a good player?"

"Not that good," Amber replied.

"I'm filing a complaint!" Mama said.

"Calm down, Baby," Daddy said to Mama. "Things like this happen sometimes in sports. Coaches have their preferences and their agendas. Amber's been lucky so far. This was bound to happen."

Mama's eyes narrowed. "So, you're good with this? We're not going to do anything?"

"No, I'm not good with this," Daddy replied. "And I think you and I need to talk about what we're going to do. In the meantime, I'd like Amber to go back to the team."

Amber's eyes went wide with shock. "What? I don't want to. I can't."

"You say this Cynthia Radcliff is not that great a player, right?"

"Right."

"What happens when she doesn't play up to par during the season? Who's going to take her place if you're not on the team?"

"Britani, I suppose," Amber said.

Daddy grinned. "You would, if you were still on the team."

Amber was not happy at that moment with Daddy. She felt the necklace warm and it startled her. She closed her eyes and the heat subsided.

"I don't know, Daddy," she finally said.

Daddy let go of her hand, then stood as he glanced at Mama.

"We're leaving it up to you, Amby," Mama said. "We'll support whatever decision you make."

"It would be a shame to see all those years of hard work go to waste," Daddy said.

"There's summer league," Amber said.

"That's true, but it's not the same," Daddy said.

"We're not going to settle anything tonight," Mama said. "Let's eat. The food is getting cold."

They sat around the table for dinner. Daddy began telling his jokes and the mood lightened. For a moment Amber forget about the day and focused on her family. She helped her parents clean the kitchen then they changed into their comfortable clothes and gathered around the coffee table in the family room to watch gameshows.

The full weight of what she'd done didn't hit her until she went to her room to do her homework. Soccer had been her passion for as long as she could remember. It took her a long time to get good at it, but once she began to fly, she soared. It was hard to imagine not playing ever again, but that's what would most likely happen if she didn't get back on the team. Like Daddy said, summer league wasn't the same. College coaches came to the high school games to recruit; they didn't pay any attention to the leagues.

Her phone buzzed and she picked it up and sighed. It was Bissau. He didn't like texting; he was old school that way. She answered.

"Hi Bissau."

"Amber! What happened? I heard you quit the soccer team. Is that true?"

"Yes it is. I quit."

"Why? Did it have something to do with the other night?"

"Yes . . . and no. Coach wants to move me to defense."

"Is that such a bad thing?" Bissau asked.

"Yes it is, especially because of the reason she's moving me."

"Cynthia Radcliff?"

"Yes! How did you know?"

"Britani told me. She said everyone was upset during practice."

Amber felt a twinge of guilt. She was a team player; what she'd done felt a bit selfish. But Coach was wrong to move her. The guilt faded.

"Well, it is what it is," she said. "Coach made a decision, and I did, too."

"What did your parents say?"

"Mama understands. Daddy is upset. I think he's going to try to talk me into going back to the team."

"Are you?"

"I don't know. I don't want to talk about that anymore."

"I understand," Bissau said. "If you want to practice on your other skills, let me know. I have some drills that might help."

"Thank you, Bissau," Amber said. "I think I'm going to chill for a while. Too many things going on. I need some time."

"Okay. Goodbye."

"Goodbye."

Amber put her phone on her dresser, then fell back onto the bed. She could see why Britani liked Bissau. He was always calm and reassuring, like an adult disguised as a teenager. It was part of his culture; he was considered an adult in Marai and had undergone initiation.

She sighed then trudged to her desk. She would concentrate on her work for now. That was the other reason for transferring. Good grades at the academy meant better college opportunities. That would be her focus for now. Soccer could wait.

CHAPTER EIGHT

Bagule turned the pages of the ancient book with care. The tome was over one hundred years old; by right, he should not have access to it. However, the djinn had been impressed by their persistence. Every day, she gave them more and more access to the museum's contents; after two weeks, they had full run of the facilities. He and Nieleni used their time efficiently, learning everything they could about Sonni Ali, Askia Muhammed, and the Songhai empire. The information was enlightening, but they had still not discovered the possible whereabouts of Sonni Ali's sword. Bagule was frustrated, but not deterred. They would find something; it was just a matter of time, and he was a very patient man.

"How goes your search?"

Bagule looked up from his book into the face of the djinn.

"Good morning, Newma. I see you have come once again to keep me company."

Newma pulled out the chair before him and sat. She placed her hands on the desk, then intertwined her fingers.

"You won't find it," she said.

"You tell me that every day, yet you allow us to keep looking. I think you believe we will."

Newma laughed. "I like to see humans waste their time. It's entertaining."

Bagule smiled. "I'm sure your entertainment will eventually come to an end."

"Would you be willing to wager on it?"

It was Bagule's turn to laugh. "That wouldn't be fair to you. I never fail."

Newma leaned closer. "You are confident. I like that. In another age, I would take you as a husband."

"Who said I would want to marry a djinn?" Bagule said.

"If I wished it to be, you wouldn't have a choice," Newma replied.

Newma's eyes locked onto his and Bagule was entranced. He wondered to himself why he'd been in her presence for so many days and never noticed her beauty. A smile came to his face as he leaned toward her.

"Marrying you would not be so bad, I think," he said.

Newma grinned. "See?"

A chill hit him and he shuddered. Bagule was confused for a moment before clarity returned. He realized what Newma had done to him and his skin warmed in anger.

"You are not as powerful as you think," Newma said as she stood. "Remember that."

Bagule glared at the djinn as she exited the room. She met Nieleni, who was coming to see Bagule. The two glanced at each other as they passed. Nieleni watched until the djinn was gone before she spoke.

"I don't like her," Nieleni said.

"Neither do I, but she is necessary for now," Bagule replied. "You have something for me?"

Nieleni's face brightened. "I decided to look at more recent sources and I found this."

Nieleni revealed a leather-bound book then placed it on the table.

"There was a robbery of the temple that held the artifacts of Sonni Ali," she said. "Many items were taken, including his sword."

Bagule's eyes widened. "Does it say who took it?

Nieleni shook her head. "No one knows for sure. Some say it was taken by local Muslims who did not consider Sonni Ali a true believer. Others say that the theft was financed by a private collector."

Bagule rubbed his chin. "If it were someone local, I think the sword would have eventually found its way back here. Who is this private collector?"

"There is no direct reference to them," Nieleni said. "However, at the time of the disappearance, the French were very powerful in this region."

"Who are the French?" Bagule replied.

"They are European. The name of their land is France."

"Then we must go to France," Bagule said.

"It is not that simple," Nieleni said. "To travel between nations, we will need certain documents that we do not possess."

"Then we will create them," Bagule said. "There are always those who are willing to do anything for the right price. We will find them."

Nieleni smiled. "Of course, we will."

Bagule stood then stretched.

"I am relieved that our time in this museum is done "

Nieleni stood as well.

"What do we do about this djinn?"

"We'll leave her be for now," Bagule said. "Once we acquire the sword, we will visit her again. Someone with as much disrespect as her needs to be taught a lesson."

"A stern lesson," Nieleni replied.

Clapping broke Bagule and Nieleni's conversation. They turned to see Newma smiling at them.

"Congratulations!" she said. "You have done more than any other person seeking that damned sword."

"I told you not to underestimate me," Bagule said.

"And you shouldn't have underestimated me," Newma replied.

Bagule tried to lift his arms, but it was too late. Nieleni managed to take one step before Newma's spell froze her in place.

"You're smarter than I thought," Newma said. "Because of this, your wish will be granted."

"What wish?" Bagule asked.

"You get to meet the Mansa."

CHAPTER NINE

Alake rubbed her hands together as she walked the halls of the compound. She worried about Amber and Bissau, and she worried about her father. Despite her powers, she felt useless. If she had only stayed when she was young and fulfilled her duties! Amber would be living a normal life and Marai would be at peace. Instead Bagule roamed the world beyond, and who knew what he was up to. By now, he surely knew the secret of the barrier, which would make him more determined and more dangerous. He had to be stopped. But was Amber powerful enough to do it?

Alake changed her direction and hurried to her Baba's chambers. She usually knocked, but such was her worry that she pushed the door open.

"Baba, I . . ."

Jakada was fully dressed and standing before his mirror. He rubbed his grizzled chin as he stared into the images flashing before him. Alake crept to his side to see what concerned him. These images were unfamiliar to her; she looked closer and her eyes widened. Her Baba was not looking into the present; he was looking into the past.

"Baba, how?" she asked.

Jakada jerked his head about, a look of surprise on his face. "Alake! What are you doing here?"

He raised his hand to wipe away the images, but Alake grabbed his wrist.

"Baba, what is this? What are you doing?"

Jakada sighed. "I guess you should know."

Alake let go of his wrist. "Know what?"

Jakada ambled to his stool as sat as the images continued to stream across the mirror.

"I believe I know what Bagule is after," he said.

Alake sat on the stool next to him. A wave of sadness washed over her briefly. This stool once belonged to her mother. Fond memories captured her.

"Alake?"

Baba's words broke her musing. When she looked to her father, he was smiling.

"I miss her every day," he said.

"I do, too," Alake said. "But we must talk of this." She gestured towards the mirror.

Jakada's smile faded.

"When Bagule was in Marai, he looked for a way to destroy the barrier from within. Now he is seeking a way to destroy it from without."

"How can he do that? He is not powerful enough."

"Not yet," Jakada said. "You and I both know the real power of the Veil."

Alake nodded.

"Now that he is free of it, I'm sure he knows, too. But that is not enough. In order to take the city, he needs allies."

"Where would he find them? The people beyond the Veil would be hard to convince."

"His *nyama* would sway many, but that is not who he seeks."

"Then who is he after?"

"He is after the djinn."

Alake's eyebrows rose. "They still exist?"

"Yes, although they have not concerned themselves with humans for ages."

Alake closed her eyes in thought.

"Why would they help Bagule? He will be a stranger to them."

"They would help him if he gave them something they desired."

"And what would that be?" Alake asked.

"The sword of Sonni Ali," Jakada said.

Alake had to think back to her early teaching to remember what Ali's sword meant to the djinn. When she finally did, fear came to her face.

"With the sword, he could control them," she said.

"Yes. And he would have his army."

Alake sprang to her feet and paced.

"What can we do?"

Jakada stood and ambled to the mirror.

"Our choices are limited. I cannot leave Marai. If I do, the Veil will falter."

"Then I will go," Alake said.

"No," Jakada replied. "I will need your help to maintain the Veil if Bagule succeeds."

"You mean to send Amber and Bissau after him," Alake said.

"Yes."

"You can't," Alake said. "Amber is still a child. She can't go roaming around the world looking for Bagule and Nieleni! Besides, what if she found them? Is she strong enough to confront them both?"

"She does not need to confront Bagule," Jakada said. "She only needs to obtain the Sword before he does. If she can find it, Bissau can bring it to us."

"She would still have to leave her home," Alake said. "That she cannot do."

"Then our only choice is to wait and hope Bagule does not find the sword," Jakada said.

They both sat again. Alake wanted to be relieved, but she wasn't. She knew Bagule; he was persistent and resourceful. He would not give up until he found the sword, if it still existed.

"I will seek the sword," Alake said.

"Did you not hear me?" Jakada said. "If Bagule finds it first and attacks the city I cannot hold him back alone."

"If he does," Alake replied. "I will return to help you, as would Amber and Bissau."

"Are you sure Amber would do so? She does not relish this responsibility."

Alake was quiet for a moment.

"I will visit her," she finally said. "As much as it pains me, I realize it is time she took on her full responsibility."

"It will change her." Jakada said. "Forever."

"I know."

"Leave as soon as you can," Jakada said.

He stood then hurried to his dresser. Opening the top drawer, he took out a small ivory box with a silver lock. He reached into his pocket and extracted a silver key, then unlocked the box. Inside was an amber necklace similar to the one she gave Amber, but larger and more elaborate. The oval amber stone was brilliant, the light inside seeming to shimmer on its own. Braided gold rimmed its edges; its cord made of woven silver and gold.

"This was your mother's," he said. "It was supposed to be yours once you became a woman. When you visit Amber, give it to her."

Alake placed her hands together. Jakada lowered the necklace into her palms and she gasped.

"Such power!" she said.

"Yes," Jakada replied. "Your mother was a formidable sonchai, much more powerful than I. She was modest when it came to her talents. It was our hope that she would one day pass this on to you."

Alake looked at her father, feeling his disappointment.

"It was not my fate," she said.

"No. It was not. But it is Amber's. The necklace will allow you to pass through the Veil. Take this to Amber. She will need it."

"I must think on this," Alake said. Amber may not be ready to handle such power.

Baba nodded.

"Do what you must, but you must decide soon. Time is running out."

CHAPTER TEN

Amber maneuvered down the crowded hallway, avoiding the glares of some of her fellow students. Soccer season had begun, and the results were not good. The girls team had three losses and no wins. For Amber, the reason was obvious: Cynthia Radcliff. But for everyone else, it was Amber's fault. If she'd remained on the team, the coach would have realized she made a mistake and switched Amber back to forward where she belonged. But with Amber off the team, that was not an option. Of course, Coach could ask her to come back, but Coach was not the type of person that would admit her mistakes publicly and Amber was not one to give her a way out.

She was on her way to her math class when she heard an adult call out her name.

"Amber?"

She turned to see Principal Stanton standing at the doorway of the school office.

"Can I have a word with you, please?"

"I'm on my way to class, Mr. Stanton," she said.

"It will only take a minute," he replied. "I'll write you a pass if it takes longer."

Amber's shoulders slumped as she trudged into the school office, following Mr. Stanton to his desk. The pale balding man sat then gestured for Amber to sit. She took her bookbag off, then eased onto the chair.

"Amber, let me start by saying that you've been a stellar student and the Academy is grateful for having you here."

"Thank you, Sir," she replied.

"Your parents have been wonderful supporters as well, although your father's golf game could use a little work."

Amber forced a smile as Mr. Stanton laughed at his joke.

Mr. Stanton leaned back in his chair and steepled his fingers.

"At the Academy, we value excellence, but what we value just as much is teamwork. It's people working together that makes us all stronger, no matter what race, religion or gender orientation. We all must work together to achieve our best."

He must be reciting a script, Amber thought.

"I agree," Amber replied.

Mr. Stanton placed his hands on his desk then leaned toward Amber.

"This is why I'm concerned about your situation with the soccer team. You are a valuable player, Amber, a true asset to the team. I was informed about your situation by Coach Sandalwood. After a long discussion, I'm happy to say that the Coach has agreed to let you return to the team."

"Will I have to play defense?" Amber asked.

"Yes," Mr. Stanton replied.

"Then I'm not interested," Amber said.

Mr. Stanton closed his eyes and took a deep breath before answering.

"Amber, sometimes we have to do things that might seem difficult in the short term to achieve our goals for the long term. You're a great player, and I think we both agree that your prospects for a soccer college scholarship are high, but not if you're not playing."

"I'm playing summer league," Amber said.

"Summer league is good, but it doesn't give you the visibility that playing at the Academy does. I believe it's one of the reasons you came here."

The necklace warmed against Amber's throat.

"I didn't want to come here," she said. "This was my parents' decision. I was looking forward to going to Jackson High School with my real friends. Ever since I've been here, I've had to change and do things I don't like to make everyone else happy. And then Coach Sandalwood makes me play defense so little Miss Cynthia can prance around for her parents."

Mr. Stanton frowned. "I don't think that's the reason . . ."

A surge of heat pulsed from the necklace into Amber. She slammed her palm on Mr. Stanton's desk, making the principal jump back.

"It is the reason!" Amber shouted.

The principal's door swung open and Ms. Pettigrew, Mr. Stanton's office manager, stepped inside.

"Is everything okay?" she asked, her narrowed eyes on Amber.

"Everything is fine," Mr. Stanton replied. "Amber seems to have lost her temper for the moment. It's understandable considering the circumstances."

Heat continued to surge from the necklace. Amber knew she must leave before she did something everyone would regret.

"I think I should wait to talk about this when I'm with my parents," she said. "I need to get to class. Can you write me a pass, Mr. Stanton?"

Mr. Stanton tore a slip of paper from his notepad, scribbled out a note then handed it to Amber.

"Be sure to tell your parents about our discussion," he said. "I'm looking forward to continuing it."

"Yes, Sir," Amber said.

She took the note and hurried from the office. When she arrived at class all eyes fell on her as she entered. She gave Mr. Means her note, then made her way to her desk. As much as she tried to focus on her work, the necklace continued to smolder. Amber finally took it off and shoved it into her backpack. By the end of the day, she was exhausted with worry. She just wanted to go home, get in the bed, and listen to music until she fell asleep.

Bissau met her at the ride pickup after school. He took one look at her and concern emanated from his eyes.

"What's the matter?" he asked.

"Remember what I did to you at your house?" she said.

"Yes," he replied.

"I was about one minute from doing it to Mr. Stanton."

Bissau's eyes widened. "What?"

"Yeah, I thought the same thing. He called me into his office and gave me this speech about responsibility and doing what you have to do and crap. He was trying to convince me to go back to the soccer team."

"And what did you say?"

"I didn't say anything," Amber said. "I was trying to keep myself from knocking him out his chair."

"I see we must work on separating your emotions from your power," he said.

"Yes. We do."

"Amber! Bissau!"

Amber and Bissau turned toward Britani sprinting to them.

"Here comes your girlfriend," Amber said.

"She is not my girlfriend," Bissau replied.

"She wants to be," Amber teased. "You should take a look at her resumé."

"I know what you're trying to do. Your jokes are not amusing."

A honking horn interrupted them. Amber's Mama pulled up into the pickup lane, waving as she climbed out of the car.

"Here's my ride," Amber said. "Meet up this weekend?"

"Sure."

Britani reached them just as Amber's mom pulled up.

"Hey girlfriend!" Britani said. "Hey, Bissau."

Amber looked at how Britani stared at Bissau and almost burst out laughing. Her eyes twinkled.

"Girlfriend," Amber said. "That's appropriate."

Bissau's eyes became slits and he frowned at her. Amber laughed. He was cute even when he was angry.

"Hello, Britani," he said without turning her way.

Britani winked at Amber as she grasped Bissau's arm and tugged it.

"Come on, Bee," she said. "We're gonna be late for practice."

Amber's eyes widened in mock surprise. "Bee? So, we got nicknames now?"

Bissau spun around then stalked away, pulling Britani with him. Britani looked over her shoulder, a big grin on her face.

"See you later, Girl!" she said.

Amber waved and laughed.

Mama appeared at her side moments later.

"Is that Bissau and Britani?" she asked.

"Yes, it is," Amber replied.

"Are they a couple now?"

"They would be if Britani had her way."

Mama put her hands on her waist. "Hmm."

Amber rolled her eyes then began walking to the car.

"Don't start, Mama," she said.

Mama hurried to catch up with her.

"I didn't say a word!"

"I know what you're thinking. Bissau and I are friends. FRIENDS."

They climbed into the car and were on their way.

"Mr. Stanton called me into his office today," Amber said.

"What?" Mama replied. "For what?"

"He's trying to talk me to going back to the soccer team. He wants to talk to you and Daddy about it."

"That's a no," Mama said. "They're not treating my baby like that then expect her to give in. That's not her way. No, it is not!"

Amber laughed. She liked when Mama went all third-person righteous.

"What will Daddy say?" Amber asked.

Mama sighed. "You know your daddy. Always trying to work out a deal. But not this time. I'll make sure of that. The only way we will even consider you going back to the team is if they reinstate you as forward."

"Yes!" Amber said. She loved it when Mama agreed with her, which these days wasn't often.

They stopped at the busy intersection between their house and the local shopping plaza.

"If this school wasn't so highly ranked, I'd pull you out," Mama said.

"Jackson High isn't so bad," Amber replied. "It's the best high school in the county."

"Don't even try it," Mama said. "That ship has sailed."

Amber slumped in her seat. It was at least worth the try.

The light turned green and Mama drove into the intersection.

"Jesus!"

Amber jerked up her head to see a blue pickup truck running the red light and hurtling at them. Her necklace flashed and she extended her hands, connecting with the truck. She grimaced as she slowed the truck, then grunted as she lifted it over the car. She twisted in her seat, keeping the truck elevated until the road cleared below it. She lowered it to the pavement, then guided the truck to the curb. Looking a few more minutes to make sure everyone was safe, she slumped in her seat clutching her necklace as she wiped sweat off her forehead.

"Amber?"

Amber looked into Mama's wide eyes.

"Oh no," Amber whispered.

"Wha . . . what just happened?"

"It's a miracle!" Amber exclaimed.

Mama didn't answer. She parked the car then ran over to the truck. The truck driver, a middle-aged white man dressed in coveralls and a flannel shirt stepped out and hugged her. They exchanged words, then Mama came back to the car. She sat in her seat, gripped the steering wheel and prayed.

"You okay, Mama?" Amber asked.

Mama stared at Amber for a moment before answering.

"I'm fine, baby. Just a little shook up." She started the car, and then drove them home. Mama kept glancing at Amber, but Amber kept her eyes ahead, hoping Mama didn't see what she'd done.

Amber didn't say a word as they entered the house. Mama placed her purse on the kitchen table, took off her coat, then sat at the table.

"Amber, sit down," she said.

Amber took off her book bag then sat. Mama reached out, taking her hands.

"We almost died today," Mama said.

Amber nodded.

Mama's expression became serious.

"We almost died, except the truck that should have hit us head on lifted into the air then landed behind us. Now we could both sit here and say it was a blessing, but I don't think it was."

Amber didn't answer. She wasn't going to say a word unless Mama asked her point blank.

"I saw your Grandma's necklace light up, and I saw you straining and sweating."

Amber remained silent.

"Baby, I'm going to ask you a question, and I want you to tell me the truth."

Amber swallowed. "Yes, Mama."

"Did you . . . no, no; there's no way you could have . . . but the truck flew over us, and your necklace. Lord, I must be going crazy."

"Mama, I . . ."

"Go on, girl," Mama said. "It's been a long week, and I must be in shock. I just thank the Lord we're alright."

Mama leaned across the table and hugged Amber.

"You go on upstairs," Mama said. "I'm going to fix me a drink."

Amber picked up her book bag and crept toward the stairs, looking back at Mama. Mama went to the cabinet and took out her bourbon and a glass, then sat down at the table and poured. Mama didn't drink often, only when she was stressed or happy. She should have told her, Amber thought. Getting it out would be somewhat of a relief. She was tired of keeping secrets; tired of all the responsibility. Maybe by telling Mama she would have someone else to share her burden. That's why she missed Grandma so much; they had no secrets between them.

She was halfway up the stairs when she hesitated. Now was the best time to tell her; she'd seen what she could do so it would be easier to accept everything. It would be the best thing.

Amber turned to head down the stairs when she heard the garage door opening. Moments later, Daddy entered the house. Mama jumped to her feet and ran to him.

"Oh baby!" she exclaimed.

Daddy dropped his briefcase then caught her in his arms.

"Baby, what's the matter? What happened?"

"Amber and I almost got killed in a car accident!"

Daddy pushed Mama away to look her in her eyes.

"What?"

Amber turned away and proceeded up the stairs. She was ready to tell Mama, but she wasn't ready for Daddy. He'd have all sorts of questions and she wasn't in the mood for an interrogation. She went to her room and got ready for bed. No homework tonight; she put on her headphones, turned on her music and lost herself in sound.

CHAPTER ELEVEN

Alake rose from her bed full of intent. All night she struggled with the thought that entered her head after he long conversation with Baba. She tried her best to come up with another solution, but there was only one way. It would change her world beyond Marai and the Veil, but she could see no other path.

She dressed quickly then went immediately Baba's chambers. The guards standing before his door bowed as she entered. Baba was sitting at his table near the balcony enjoying a bowl of sorghum. He looked up at her and began to smile until he noticed her stern look. His smile faded.

"What is it, Alake?" he asked.

"I must go," she said.

Baba lowered his head.

"Then we both have come to the same conclusion."

Alake sat opposite of Baba. A servant brought her a bowl of sorghum, but she waved him away.

"Amber will not take what we do seriously unless I'm there," she said.

"I agree," Baba replied. "But what of your daughter? How will she handle this?"

"Very badly at first," Alake said. "She is her father's daughter. But she will accept it. She has no choice."

Alake looked into her Baba's eyes. "I don't think Amber is ready for Mama's necklace. She must master what she possesses."

"So be it. We must prepare," Baba said. "You must use the mirror, of course."

Alake nodded.

"The question is, where will you go?" he asked.

"I know of someone who will welcome us."

Baba pushed his bowl away.

"Then let us prepare."

Alake and Baba went to his mirror. Baba reached into his chest and took out two pouches of powder. He gave one to Alake. She opened the pouch then nodded. Baba opened the second pouch and poured a small amount of the powder in his left hand. He touched the mirror with his right hand and the surface swirled in response.

"To Amber," he said.

He blew the powder into the mirror, then stepped aside. The mirror surface stabilized, revealing the dark interior of Amber's room. Alake shared a smile, then stepped into the mirror. Seconds later, she stood in Amber's room at the foot of her bed. Amber was fast asleep with her earbuds. Alake smiled; she'd grown so much since she last saw her. She gave Amber a few more moments of peace before kneeling beside her bed.

"Amber," she whispered. "Wake up. It's Grandma."

Amber shifted.

"No, it's not," she whispered back, her eyes still closed. "Grandma's in Marai."

Alake almost laughed. *Always difficult, even in her sleep.* She touched Amber's shoulder.

"No baby girl," she replied. "I'm right here in your bedroom."

Amber's eyes popped open. She jerked her head toward Alake and a smile broke on her face like the sun.

"Grandma!"

Alake warmed seeing Amber's eyes.

"Hello, Amber."

Amber sat up, her joyous expression melting into a concerned frown.

"What are you doing here?"

Alake's joy faded as well.

"Amber, you must go with me."

"Where . . . wait, I can't! I have to go to school tomorrow!"

"It won't take long; we're travelling through the mirrors and I know exactly where we need to go."

"Where?" Amber asked.

"To Senegal. To Miss Josephine's house."

Amber swallowed. "Do I have to go?"

"Yes. Whatever we find there will be for you to see."

"Amber?"

Alake and Amber both looked at her door.

"Hide!" Amber said.

Alake dropped to the floor then scrambled under the bed. Moments later, Amber's door open. The voice she heard made her smile despite her awkward situation.

"Baby girl, who are you talking to in here? I know you're not on that phone this time of night."

"Mama, you know we don't use the phone to talk," Amber said. "I must have been talking in my sleep."

The bed pressed down as her daughter sat on it.

"Can you believe what happened today?" she said.

"No, I can't," Amber said. "We were lucky."

"No, that wasn't luck. That was like you said. It was a miracle."

Her daughter stood, relieving Alake from the pressure.

"It's been a while since we been to church," her daughter said. "We're going this weekend."

"Yes, Mama," Amber said.

"Your daddy is going to, whether he likes it or not. Ain't nobody too busy for the Lord."

Her daughter left the room. Alake wanted to see her so bad, but it was not the time. Not yet. She crawled from under the bed.

"What happened today?" she asked.

Amber ran her hand across her head.

"Mama and I were on our way home when a truck veered toward us. It was about to hit us head on, but I lifted it over us then sat it down on the other side of the street."

Alake was proud and concerned at the same time.

"Your Mama saw it all?"

"Yeah. She looked at me funny, and I blurted that it was a miracle. She jumped on that."

"I think we will have to tell her soon," Alake said. "Your father, too. Things are happening fast, and it will be harder for you to keep hidden who you are from those close to you."

"I'm not ready to tell Daddy yet," Amber said. "He'll freak out."

Alake smiled. "Then he'll have to. Now get dressed. We must go."

Amber climbed out of the bed, then went to her closet. She dressed casual, a pair of jeans, a pullover shirt, and a light jacket. She turned to face Alake, a worried expression on her face.

I'm ready," she said.

Alake held out her hand and Amber took it. Together they approached the mirror. Alake took the powder from her pocket, then blew it on the mirror. They waited until the surface shimmered, then together they stepped through.

* * *

Josephine stood at the bottom of the stairway, a worried look on her face. The deliverymen eased their way down, careful to keep the heavy dresser high above the railings. The stairway and the dresser were antiques and it would be a tragedy if either were marred. Josephine had no doubt in the men's strength; both were wrestlers, a fact displayed by their broad shoulders and thick arms. What she doubted was their precision.

One of the deliverymen stumbled. Josephine gasped as the dresser leg came close to the railing, but at the last minute the young wrestler lifted the leg to safety.

"Careful, *mes ames!*" she said. "Careful!"

The men looked at each other and shook their heads. Josephine knew she was being a pain, but these were valuable items.

The men finally reached the bottom of the stairs. Josephine led them to her antiques room to a spot cleared for the dresser. The men sat the item down and Josephine sighed with relief.

"Excellent job," she said. She went into her purse and pulled out their tip. The looks on their face showed their pleasure.

"Good luck in your matches tomorrow," she said.

"Will you be there?" one of the men asked.

"Unfortunately, no," Josephine replied. "I must prepare for new guests. It is the Year of the Return, is it not?"

The other man frowned. "I don't see the big deal."

"You are not African American," Josephine replied.

"And you are?" he retorted.

"Don't be rude, Amadou," the other man said. "Ms. Josephine just tipped us a week's pay."

Amadou nodded. "You are right. I apologize, Ms. Josephine."

Josephine waved her hand. "Think nothing of it. Everyone is entitled to their opinion. Now off you go. I have work to do."

The men made their way to the front door and let themselves out. Josephine watched them climb into the delivery truck and drive away before returning to the antiques room.

"I like what you've done," a woman said.

Josephine shrieked as she jumped back. Two women stood in her foyer, both smiling.

"Don't be afraid," the older woman said. "Has it been so long that you don't recognize us?"

Josephine squinted, then a smile came to her face.

"Alake? Amber? Is that you?"

Alake grinned as she walked toward Josephine, her arms wide.

"Yes, it's us."

Josephine and Alake embraced; Amber stepped in and joined.

"Hi Miss Josephine," Amber said.

"It is you!" Josephine said. Josephine let go of Alake then took a moment to gaze at Amber. "Look at you! When I last saw you, you were a child. Now you are a woman. You are so beautiful!

Amber blushed. "I'm not a woman yet. But I am beautiful."

The three of them laughed.

Josephine's heart was full of joy. "I am so happy to see you! I was beginning to think that entire episode was a dream."

"It wasn't," Alake said.

Josephine grabbed their hands and led them into the foyer.

"Come now, we must catch up. You must tell me everything!"

Alake stopped, pulling Josephine still.

"I wish we had time, but we don't. We have come for an urgent matter. We've come to use your mirror."

Dread consumed Josephine's thoughts as she clasped her lapis lazuli necklace. She'd worn the talisman ever since the day the true purpose of the antique mirror was revealed by Bissau's visit.

"I . . .I don't know," Josephine said. "That thing is evil."

Alake grasped Josephine's hand and smiled.

"It is neither good nor evil," Alake said. "It's a tool; a special tool, but a tool, nonetheless. It takes on the personality of the person using it, and we will not use it to harm. We seek knowledge that only the mirror can share."

Josephine's eyes shifted between Alake and Amber. When they last visited, they had brought trouble with them. Now they were here again. Was trouble far behind? She sighed, lifting her shoulders in an exaggerated motion. Despite their strangeness, she liked them both.

"Come with me," she said.

Josephine led them to her bedroom.

"Did you notice the changes?" she asked. She was small talking, something she did when she was nervous or afraid.

"No, I didn't," Alake answered.

"I decided to freshen things up. The house had become so drab. I needed something new."

"Are you still renting?" Amber asked.

"Not as much," Josephine replied. "Ever since my butler quit, I haven't been able to replace him. Renting is too much work for one person."

They entered the room and Josephine went directly to her jewel box. She opened it and took out two keys.

"Now we're ready," she said. "Follow me."

Josephine opened the door and they entered. The furniture was covered with dust cloths, all except the mirror. It stood near the wall reflecting their approach. Amber stopped for a moment. She noticed a bluish-green light emanating from the glass.

"Do you see it?" Amber asked her grandmother.

"Barely," she replied. "Not a much you, I suspect."

"See what?" Josephine asked.

"Nothing," Amber and her grandmother said together.

They walked to the mirror, then stopped. Grandma turned to Josephine, then smiled.

"Miss Josephine, I know this your home, but I must ask you for some time alone with Amber. There are things that will happen here that is best you do not see."

"Gladly," Josephine said. She scurried away, closing the door behind her.

Alake waited for a moment before reaching into her pocket and taking out a powder bag.

"Where are we going?" Amber asked.

"To the past," Alake replied.

Alake took a pinch of powder from the pouch, then blew it on the mirror. The reflective surface simmered like a lake disturbed by a stone, then wavered like shifting tides. Alake's eyes narrowed before she spoke.

"Show me Sonni Ali," she said.

The mirror surface spun like a tempest and dizziness struck them both. They stumbled sideways, almost falling. Amber grabbed Alake, regaining her balance as they returned to the mirror. Images swirled in the magical maelstrom as the mirror took them further and further back in time. After a few more minutes, the swirling slowed, and the mirror shimmered again. Amber saw a desert, filled with people . . . no, an army. Leading this army was a man wearing an elaborate turban and exquisite robes.

"Sonni Ali," Alake whispered.

To their surprise, the man turned his head to them, then smiled. Amber jumped away. Could he see her?

Sonni Ali reached down to his side and extracted his sword from its gilded scabbard. It was a beautiful blade, crafted by the best blacksmiths in Songhai. He raised the blade overhead and his army cheered upon seeing it. But something else happened as well. A peculiar cloud formed over the army, one that did not threaten the rain that was so rare and precious in the region. This was a cloud of a different origin. Alake studied it closer; she could make out faces, countenances that grimaced like prisoners trapped.

"Djinn," Alake whispered.

The image disappeared, replace by the interior of a room. Amber heard the muffled sound of footfalls on carpet, then a low light illuminated the room. In the background was a display of weapons from around the world, some she recognized, others she did not. Before them all, sequestered in a glass case, was the same sword Sonni Ali held.

"That is what we seek," Alake said to Amber. "The sword of Sonni Ali."

"Why?" Amber asked.

"Bagule wants it," Alake replied. "It has something to do with the djinn. What, I do not know."

"Can the mirror tell us where it is?" Amber asked.

Alake put her hands close to the glass. She tried to press against it.

"Ahhh!"

She jerked her hands away in obvious pain.

"Grandma!"

Amber reached for Alake, but she waved her away.

"I'm okay. I was more surprised than hurt." She looked at Amber.

"You try."

Amber's eyes went wide.

"To go through?"

Alake nodded. "Yes."

"But I'm not sure where I'm going."

"You have to try," Alake urged. "It's very important that we get this sword before Bagule does."

Amber lifted her hands, then stepped toward the mirror. The light she saw earlier reappeared and increased in intensity as her hands neared the glass. She touched it and felt a calming presence flow into her. There was a flash, and she stared into the solemn face of Sonni Ali.

"A child of power," he said, his voice deep and resolute. He did not speak English, yet Amber understood him.

"This is what you seek, and it will do what you wish. But it will not be this easy."

Sonni Ali threw his head back and laughed. An invisible force shoved Amber away from the mirror, causing her to stumble then fall on her backside. Alake came to her side then helped her up.

"What happened?" she asked.

"Sonni Ali spoke to me," Amber said. "He told me we need the sword, but he wouldn't let me through."

"You'll have to go where it is to obtain it."

"And where is that?" Amber asked.

"You'll know when it's time," Alake answered. She took Amber's hand.

"We are done," she said. I must get you back home before your parents miss you."

When they opened the door to the room Josephine was waiting.

"Is it done?" she asked. "Is it over?"

"It is for now," Alake replied.

Josephine rolled her eyes. "When will it be over for good?"

"We cannot say," Alake answered. "But we thank you for your help. We will leave you now. Thank you so much."

"How will you leave?" Josephine asked. "How did you get here?"

"Through your bedroom mirror," Alake replied.

"Oh my God!" Josephine's hands flew to her mouth. "Is my mirror haunted too?"

Alake laughed. "It's not haunted. All mirrors are portals, some more than others."

They went to Josephine's mirror. Amber hugged Josephine.

"Goodbye Miss Josephine," she said. "I hope the next time I'm here it's just for vacation."

"I hope so too, sweetheart."

Alake blew the powder into the mirror and they entered the swirling void. When they finally reached Amber's room they bumped into something hard. It took Amber's eyes a moment to adjust. Standing before her with wide eyes was her mother.

"Amber?"

"Mama?"

Amber's mother looked at Grandma.

"Mama?"

"Baby?"

Amber's mother's eyes rolled back into her head and she fainted.

CHAPTER TWELVE

Bagule's eyes blinked from the sand blown into his face by the brisk warm wind. Nieleni dropped her head as low as she could to avoid the deluge. Before them, a barren mountain range loomed, rising from the surrounding sand like a ragged snow-capped wall.

"It's beautiful, isn't it?"

Newma's face was locked in a wistful gaze at the summits. Bagule did not know how they arrived at the base of the peaks; he blacked out right after Newma said they were to meet the djinn Mansa. His arms were still locked to his sides, as were Nieleni's.

"What are we waiting for?" Nieleni asked. "Take us inside!"

Newma laughed. "The lackey wants to give orders now?"

"When my hands are free, I will strangle you to death!" Nieleni shouted.

"I won't take you inside. This is as far as I go," Newma said, ignoring Nieleni's threat. "Alas, I am not allowed into the kingdom. We djinn have our place, and mine is not within."

"What about us?" Bagule asked.

"The Mansa has been informed of your arrival. Someone will come for you . . . eventually."

"Then give us our hands," Bagule said. "We should be able to defend ourselves."

"You are in the land of Djinn," Newma replied. "You will be safe until our Mansa summons you."

Newma ambled to Bagule.

"Remember, you asked for this," she said. "Do not doubt now."

Newma laughed. Her image shimmered, then blew away with the wind.

"Ahhhh!" Nieleni shrieked.

"Save your anger," Bagule advised. "Nothing we do will change our situation."

"We could die here," she replied.

"We won't," Bagule said. "Newma did not bring us here on her own. We were summoned. I'm sure we're being watched."

Nieleni grunted. She jerked about in an attempt to free her arms.

"Rest, Nieleni," Bagule said. "We must conserve our energy for what's to come."

"Whatever that will be," Nieleni replied.

Bagule glanced at his companion, her last words finding purchase in his thoughts. For the first time since escaping Marai he was uncertain. Every step they had taken since that fateful day had been planned and executed by him. The outcomes had been weighed and anticipated. But this was different. The djinn turned out to be more powerful than he anticipated. There was a time to act, and a time to observe. Now was the time to observe.

The sun took its time crossing the open sands, finally seeking refuge below the western horizon. The heat that had battered Bagule and Nieleni throughout the day fled with the sunlight, leaving a chilly void in its wake. Hunger and thirst had come and gone, leaving both of them weak. As the last light faded, a mist formed about the base of the mountains, rising and condensing until the peaks were barely visible. The mist crept across the sands, eventually reaching and overtaking Bagule and Nieleni. Bagule was barely conscious when he felt the moisture sting his exposed skin. The invisible grip around his arms subsided, but he was too weak to notice. He fell and was caught by the now dense mist swirling about him like a small tempest. Bagule managed to look toward Nieleni. She was prone, hovering a few feet above the ground, looking as if she slept on a cloud. Together, they drifted toward the mountains.

A gilded door appeared as they reached the base of the natural citadel. The door opened and light streamed from a mysterious source. Bagule drifted inside, followed by Nieleni. The darkness gave way to brilliant light. Bagule raised his head and was astounded. The kingdom of the djinn spread out before him; wide avenues lighted with mystical lamps hovering above the brick paved streets. Djinn filled the streets, some in human form, others in bizarre combinations of human and animal pairings, more in translucent shapes. As they were lowered to the ground a pink cloud drifted toward them. Bagule felt his limbs relax and he stood. Nieleni came to his side, her eyes wide as she looked at the strangeness surrounding them.

"Welcome to the Djinn kingdom," the pink cloud said. "I am Farheen, advisor to the Mansa. Please follow me. She is expecting you."

Farheen drifted away. Bagule hesitated, then followed. Nieleni lagged behind him, studying every being she encountered.

"I don't how to kill some of these things," she muttered.

"Let's hope that's not a challenge you'll have to deal with," Bagule replied.

"I can assure you're in no danger," Farheen said. "You are here under Newma's protection."

"What makes Newma so special?" Nieleni asked.

"She is the Mansa's daughter," Farheen replied.

Another detail the djinn decided to leave out, Bagule mused. He would have to be extra cautious with these djinns. Apparently, their words were not to be trusted.

Their journey ended before a palace of the likes of which Bagule had never seen. The gold encrusted stone walls towered as high as the grandest castle, and the moat was as wide as the sea.

The bridge spanning the moat was created with ebony wood, with a wrought iron railing stretching the entire length.

"You expect us to walk that far?" Nieleni asked.

"No," Farheen replied. "Someone will come for us soon. It would save us time if you gave me your weapons now."

Nieleni flinched as if hit. Bagule grinned.

"Do as it asks," Bagule said.

Nieleni frowned, then extracted her various blades.

"Oh my!" Farheen exclaimed.

"One must be prepared," Nieleni replied.

As Nieleni handed over her last knife, their exchange was interrupted by a strange sight. A chariot arrived to take them to the other side of the moat, and it was nothing like Bagule had seen. The body of the vehicle was similar to the craft used by the ancient Egyptians. Pulling the chariot were two of the largest horses Bagule had ever seen. There seemed to be no charioteer, but Bagule knew better by now. He saw the reins tightened and his suspicions were confirmed.

"Come," Bagule said to Nieleni. "We mustn't keep the Mansa waiting."

Bagule and Nieleni climbed into the chariot. The vehicle turned then sped across the bridge faster than Bagule thought possible, even in the modern vehicles he and Nieleni had used since leaving Marai. When they reached the other side, the chariot stopped and the rear gate swung open.

"Follow the red path," the bodyless charioteer said. "The Mansa is waiting."

Bagule and Nieleni did not see a path.

"There is no path here!" Nieleni said.

The transparent charioteer laughed.

"There will be as soon as you start walking."

Bagule took the lead. Three steps into his journey, the path appeared, illuminating a thick garden filled with brilliant flowers. The competing fragrances from the blooms were intoxicating and distracting, as they were meant to be. Both Bagule and

Nieleni found it difficult to concentrate on their journey, so distracting was the ornate fauna. Several times they found themselves enamored by a particular flower and had to break themselves way.

Finally, they reached the entrance to the Mansa's palace. The towering thick doors were opened and there were no guards. They entered, stepping onto a thick, narrow rug that swallowed their shoes. At the end of the carpet, sitting in a massive throne, was the Mansa. To say that she was beautiful would have been insulting. Never had Bagule seen a person so perfect. Her ebony skin accented the bright colors of her robe and headwrap. Golden bracelets of various thicknesses encircled her wrists; jeweled rings adorned each finger.

"She's perfect," Nieleni said, her voice filled with awe. Neither of them could find the strength to approach.

"Come now," she said, her booming voice filling the wide atrium. "I've been expecting you for some time."

Bagule bowed. "It was the garden, my Mansa. It can be rather captivating."

"As it was designed to be," the Mansa replied. "There are djinn who are still there after hundreds of years, wandering through its beauty. But you are humans. You don't appreciate such things."

Bagule and Nieleni proceeded to the Mansa. The carpet tugged at their feet; by the time they reached the Mansa they were exhausted.

"You have so many distractions," Bagule said.

"No one can never be sure if those approaching them are friends or foe," the Mansa replied. "We djinn are a deceitful lot."

"Are you deceiving us now?" Bagule asked.

The Mansa laughed. "We will see. My daughter said you think you know where Sonni Ali's enchanted sword is hidden."

"I think I do," Bagule said.

"Where?"

Bagule grinned. "That is my secret."

"So, you have come to the center of the djinn realm to barter with me? That was foolish."

"I don't think so," Bagule said. "In my research, I discovered something very interesting about Sonni Ali's sword."

The Mansa's flawless smile faded. "Did you, now?"

Bagule nodded. "Sonni Ali was not only a great leader, but he was also a powerful sorcerer. Legends say that his sword can only be held by human hands. Any djinn that touches the handle will be sucked inside it and trapped forever."

The Mansa was silent, her face distorted with anger.

"I also learned something else."

"What is that?"

"If the sword is freely given to a djinn, the djinn can possess it and free those trapped inside. Of course, with that done, the sword loses its powers."

The Mansa tilted her head.

"What are you proposing, Bagule?"

"I will find this sword. When I do, I will give it to you. I have no need of such things."

The Mansa scratched her chin. "And what do you want in return."

"I need an army of djinn," Bagule said.

"For what?"

"To free the city of Marai from the clutches of Jakada."

The Mansa sat up in her throne, her eyes wide.

"Marai still exists! How do you know this!"

"Because Nieleni and I escaped it. But to return, we must penetrate the Veil that has hidden it from the world for centuries. With your djinn, I can do it."

"Bring me the sword and an army you shall have," the Mansa said.

"As soon as I locate the sword, I will."

"I know where the sword is," the Mansa said.

Bagule was caught off guard by the Mansa's revelation. The Mansa beamed.

"We have always known," the Mansa continued. "But it has done us no good, since we could not possess it. We watched it, hoping to keep any other human from finding it to use against us."

"Tell me and it is yours," Bagule said.

"It is kept in a private antique collection in a city called London."

"Then I will go and claim it," Bagule said. "There is one more thing."

"Yes?"

"There is a person that could interfere with my plans. I need her out of the way."

The Mansa leaned toward Bagule.

"Who is this person?"

""Her name is Amber."

CHAPTER THIRTEEN

Amber and her Grandmother managed to lift her Mother from the floor onto her bed. She looked at Grandma, her worry showing on her face.

"You should go," she said. "I think I can handle this."

"How?" Grandma asked. "By telling her she didn't see what she obviously saw? No. It's time we told her. It's time she knew. It will make it easier on you for things to come."

Amber's throat went dry.

"What things?"

Mama stirred, then opened her eyes. She looked at Amber then smiled.

"Hey, baby. What just happened?"

"You fainted, Mama," Amber answered.

"Why would I faint? I heard sounds coming from your room and I came to check on you then I saw you . . ."

"You saw us emerge from Amber's mirror," Grandma said.

Mama sat up straight with fear in her eyes.

"Who the. . . Mama?"

Grandma smiled. "Yes, baby. It's me."

"But it can't be! My Mama is in Africa, and she's older than you. You look younger than me!"

"It's me, Peaches."

Amber and Mama's eyes widened.

"Peaches?" Amber said. "You called her Peaches?"

"I used to call her that when she was very young," Grandma said. "She asked me to stop when she turned twelve. She said she was a woman now and couldn't be called by some silly nickname. I kept calling her that until she was eighteen."

Mama scooted away from them to the head of Amber's bed.

"Only my Mama and daddy would know that. What in the world is going on?"

Grandma followed her. She sat beside her and stroked her hair. Mama seemed to calm down, the fear in her eyes fading.

"It's really you, Mama?"

"Yes, it is, Baby. Remember those stories I used to try to tell you that you thought were boring? Amber listened."

"So, it was all true?" Mama asked.

Grandma nodded. "All of it."

"What does that have to do with you and Amber stepping out of a mirror and you looking like you just graduated from college?"

"Well . . ."

"Crystal, you seen my socks?"

Mama jumped hearing Daddy's voice.

"I'll be right back," she said.

"Mama, please don't tell daddy!" Amber pleaded.

"Tell your daddy? Do I look crazy?" She looked at Grandma. "Well, I might be, but the last thing I'll do is tell him. I'll be back. Promise."

"You think she'll tell him?" Amber asked Grandma.

"No," Grandma replied. "Your daddy is a conservative man when it comes to things like this. He wouldn't believe the moon was falling until it fell on him. Then he would consider it."

Amber burst out laughing then covered her mouth.

"Grandma!"

"Is Amber awake?" her father asked.

"She's doing some last-minute homework," Mama replied.

"Let me give her a kiss before I go," Daddy asked.

"Here's your socks. And don't go up there disturbing her. She's not five."

"She'll always be my baby."

"That's sweet; now go to work. I'm right behind you."

"Love you."

"Love you, too."

Amber heard the back door close and the garage door lift and close. Moments later, her door opened, and Mama stepped inside. She looked at Amber and Grandma then sighed.

"I don't know what to say," she said.

"Sit," Grandma said. "I'll explain everything."

Mama sat as she was told and Grandma shared everything, from her childhood and the day she decided to flee Marai, to the day she and Amber were summoned, to the moment they stepped out of the mirror and were discovered by Mama. Mama listened, her eyes shifting back and forth between them and the mirror.

"Why don't I have these abilities?" Mama asked.

"Because you did not want them," Grandma replied.

Mama folded her arms across her chest. "If you would have just told me straight, I might have."

Grandma closed her eyes for a minute.

"Uh oh," Amber said. Grandma was choosing her words. That was not good.

"That's not how it works," she finally said. "A person must come to these abilities freely. They cannot be given to you or forced upon you. You must believe in them for them to manifest within you."

Grandma stood. "I must go now, and you to must be about your day. We will speak again."

"When?" Mama asked.

"Tonight," Grandma replied.

Grandma went to the mirror. She took out her pouch, poured a bit of powder in her hand, then blew it at the mirror. The glass shimmered.

"Tonight, my babies," she said. She stepped into the mirror. Mama fell back onto the bed.

"How am I supposed to go to work after this? This is too much!"

Amber pulled at Mama's arm.

"Come on, let's go. I can't miss school. We can talk on the way."

Mama sat up.

"And you know we will. How could you keep this secret from me? I'm your Mama!"

"Grandma told me to, and she outranks us both," Amber replied.

Mama finally stood.

"I'm going to go get dressed. Still don't see how y'all expect me to work after this."

She left Amber's room. Amber collapsed on her bed, then slapped her forehead. Grandma said it was good Mama knew. They would have to sneak around less, and there were things that had to be done that required at least one of her parents knowing.

Amber forced herself off the bed, dressed for school, then trudged downstairs to wait for Mama. She appeared moments later, a semi-dazed look on her face.

"Okay Baby, let's go," she said.

"Mama, are you sure you're okay?"

"No, I'm not okay, but I'm going to work, and you're going to school, so let's go."

They climbed into Mama's car then headed to Amber's school. Mama turned the radio to the old school station.

"So, can you fly?" she asked.

"What?" Amber replied.

"Can you fly? You know, like Superman?"

"It's not like that," Amber said. "I'm not a superhero."

"That's right. Mama said it was some kind of magic."

"Yeah, something like that," Amber replied.

"Do you have a magic wand or something?'

Amber reached into her blouse and pulled out her necklace. "I have this," she said.

"Your amber necklace! It's magic?"

"Yeah, sort of."

"So how does it work?"

"I'm not sure," Amber replied. "It focuses my energy."

"So, what can you do?"

"I can sense people's emotions and how they really feel."

"What else?"

"I can move things."

"Move things?"

"I can pick up things without touching them."

"So you can . . ."

Mama slammed on the brakes. Amber threw out her hand instinctively, but the seat belt kept her from crashing into the dashboard.

"That truck the other day!" Mama exclaimed. "That wasn't a miracle. That was *you!*"

Amber nodded. "Mama, we're stopped in the middle of the road."

"What?"

A shrill chorus of car horns broke Mama's trance.

"Okay, okay!" she shouted.

Mama continued driving.

"We have a lot to talk about. A whole lot," she said.

Amber was relieved to see the school. Mama pulled up to the curb and Amber jumped out.

"Tonight, after your daddy goes to sleep. Okay?"

"Okay," Amber said.

Amber climbed out of the car. She was already exhausted, and school hadn't started yet. She looked up to see Bissau sauntering toward her, a pleasant smile on his face. She was happy to see him.

"Hi Amber," he said.

"You won't believe what happened last night," she replied. "Grandma came to see me from Marai!"

Bissau's pleasant demeanor faded.

"Why was I not told?"

"I don't know."

Bissau frowned. "I should have been informed."

"I don't know why you weren't," Amber replied. "Anyway, we went to Senegal, to Miss Josephine's house."

"What?!?" Bissau was clearly upset. "You went back to use her mirror. Why?"

"Grandma said we had to use it to look back in time to find Sonni Ali's sword."

"And did you?"

"Yes. It's somewhere in New York. But that's not the crazy part."

Bissau's eyes narrowed. "What else happened?"

"When we came back to my room, my Mama was there."

Bissau closed his eyes, then lowered his head.

"And now she knows everything."

"Yep."

When Bissau lifted his head, he was smiling.

"This is a good thing. It was bound to happen."

"That's what Grandma said," Amber replied.

"What about your Baba?"

"No, no, no," Amber replied. "We're going to need a little more time before we tell him. Or maybe we won't tell him at all."

"It's not fair for your Mama to know and not your Baba."

Amber laughed. "This has nothing to do with fairness. My 'Baba' would not handle this well at all."

"Amber! Bee!"

Amber and Bissau turned to see Britani jogging toward them.

"Here comes your girlfriend," Amber said.

"She's not my girlfriend," Bissau replied.

"She will be. She's determined. She's even wearing makeup. Your days are numbered."

Britani inserted herself between them, a big smile on her face.

"What are y'all up to?" she asked.

"Nothing, girl," Amber said. "I'm just on my way to homeroom. Bissau was waiting to walk you to yours."

"What?"

Britani grabbed Bissau's arm and began pulling him away.

"We'll talk later Amber," Britani said with a wink.

Amber waved. "See ya!"

Amber giggled as she walked away. She allowed her vision to come forward. Britani radiated bright pink, full of positive emotion. Bissau was a light blue, which surprised her. She expected him to be a cool blue based on what he said, but it looked like he was actually beginning to like Britani. Amber didn't know how she felt about that. She shook her head, then laughed.

"Look at you, girlfriend," she said to herself. "Didn't want the boy when he wanted you, now you're confused."

It was another dull day at school. The soccer season ended in disaster; Coach Sandalwood's grand strategy went down in flames. Amber felt sorry for Cynthia; she tried her best, but she just wasn't good enough. A few of the team members blamed Amber, but Amber didn't care. She still loved soccer, but she didn't love soccer at the academy. Her mind was focused on summer league and playing with her real friends.

The day passed by faster than normal because she was dreading her conversation with Mama. She waited as patiently as she could for Mama to arrive, patting her foot on the pavement and humming with the song playing on her phone. She was so into the tune that Bissau's hand on her shoulder startled her.

"Hey!" she said.

She turned to see Bissau hovering two feet over the ground, his eyes wide. Amber put him down immediately then hugged him.

"I'm so sorry!" she said.

Bissau hugged her back. For a moment, they held each other, a smile coming to Amber's face. This felt good. She finally let him go. She caught a brief smile from Bissau before it was replaced with a frown.

"We really have to work on your control," he said.

"Yeah, I know. I will."

"You should tell your mother about me as well," he said. "That way we can train together without sneaking around."

"That would be easy," she replied. "She thinks you should be my boyfriend."

"That's a good idea," Bissau said.

"Hold on, Bee," Amber said, deliberately using Britani's nickname for him. "I think you're missing a few steps to making that happen."

Bissau looked confused. "What are you . . . ah, no. I'm not saying your real boyfriend. If your Mama thinks I am your boyfriend, it will be natural for us to spend more time together."

"But if I tell her who you are, we won't have to do the boyfriend-girlfriend thing."

"That is true," Bissau said.

Amber looked at his aura. He was disappointed.

"But maybe we could do it for my daddy. He doesn't know yet, and I hope he never knows."

Bissau smiled again.

"That would work."

"So, what are you going to do about Britani?" Amber asked.

"Nothing. She is not my girlfriend."

"But what if it gets out that you and I are dating?"

"But we're not."

"You just said we were."

"We are, but not really."

"So, what do we call this?"

Bissau stopped to consider until he saw the smirk on Amber's face. He shook his fist at her.

"Why do you tease me like this?" he said.

Amber laughed loud.

"Because it's fun and you're easy."

Bissau threw his hand up.

"Sometimes I wish this was over."

"But we just started dating!" Amber crooned.

Bissau turned and stomped away.

"Goodbye, Amber."

"Goodbye, Bee!"

Amber laughed as Bissau stalked away. That was wrong to do, but teasing Bissau relieved the tension. Mama pulled up as she turned back towards the parking lot. Amber opened the back door and tossed her backpack onto the seat. She jumped into the car on the passenger side.

"How are you, Mama?" she asked.

"I'm confused," she said. "But I'm getting there."

"You can ask me anything," Amber said. "I'll answer what I can."

"Before I do that, I heard from your Aunt Terry. Her and your uncle are going on a cruise this summer and they want to know if Harriet can stay with us while they're gone. She asked to see her cousin Amber."

"That might be complicated," Amber said. "But I would love to see Harriet. The last time I saw her, she was eight."

"We're their last chance," Mama said.

"I guess it's okay," Amber said.

"Good."

Mama pulled out of the parking lot and into traffic.

"So how did my Mama get so young?" she asked.

"I'm not sure," Amber said. "She said something about Marai is selfish with its time."

"Marai?"

"That's where Grandma is from," Amber explained. "It's a city in Africa, Mali, I think. It's hidden from the rest of the world by magic."

Mama stared at Amber.

"And this is true?"

Amber nodded. "It is. I've been there."

"So how did she get to America?"

"That's kind of complicated, too," Amber said. "I think you should talk to Grandma."

"I will," Mama said. "I can't believe she hid this from all of us, even daddy!"

"Would you have believed her if she told you?" Amber asked.

"No," Mama confessed. "No I wouldn't have. But still . . ."

"I wasn't sure until I saw great-granddaddy in my mirror."

"What does he look like?"

"I'm sure you'll find out soon, now that everything is out."

Mama steered the car into the driveway.

"We have got to keep this away from your daddy," she said.

"I know," Amber replied.

"That man would blow a gasket. Hopefully you can do whatever you need to do quickly so it won't come up."

"I hope so," Amber replied. "I really do."

CHAPTER FOURTEEN

Bagule walked down the aisle of the airplane on shaky legs. To say he was relieved the flight was over was an understatement. Nieleni strolled in front of him, completely unphased. Bagule decided he would have to devise another way to travel between lands, one that did not depend on the unstable devices built by questionable hands.

He regained his confidence as they ambled through the terminal. Nieleni suggested they carry nothing with them so they would not be delayed acquiring their baggage in case it was lost. They would purchase whatever they needed once they settled. She studied the process as she always did, allowing Bagule to concentrate on more important things. In this case, it was finding Sonni Ali's sword.

They exited the terminal into the damp London air. Bagule frowned; he was not accustomed to so much moisture, and he had no intention of becoming so. The airport bustled with people, the roads crowded with vehicles of all types, the atmosphere tainted with the stench of chemicals.

"This is not a pleasant place," he said.

"I agree," Nieleni replied.

She stepped close to the curb to hail a taxi.

"That won't be necessary."

Bagule and Nieleni turned to see a stout Black man in a tailored suit sauntering toward them. The man wore a derby hat and carried a black umbrella in his left hand. He stopped before Bagule and bowed.

"Welcome to London!" he said. "I'm Ephraim Coleman. I'll be your guide during your stay."

Nieleni stepped between Bagule and the man, eyeing him up and down.

"Are you a djinn?" she asked.

"No," Ephraim replied. "However, my family has a long history with them."

"Then why are you doing this?" she asked.

"Our association with the djinn has been quite beneficial," Ephraim answered. "It's been quite some time since they have asked for our assistance. It seems they have no direct contact here. Besides, who would turn down a request from the Djinn Mansa?"

"Where is the Sword of Sonni Ali," Bagule asked.

"Well, you're don't waste time, do you," Ephraim said.

"Well, where it is?" Nieleni asked.

"I don't know," Ephraim replied.

"Then you are of no use to us, and the Mansa lied," Bagule said.

"Here's the thing," Ephraim said. "Even if there was a djinn or two here, they wouldn't be able to locate the sword. It is invisible to them."

"The Mansa didn't tell us that," Bagule said.

"I'm not surprised," Ephraim said. "Djinn are quite proud. They don't like admitting their shortcomings, especially the Mansa."

Ephraim looked around them.

"No bags," he said.

"We're traveling light," Nieleni replied.

"Excellent. It will save us time. I'll get you checked in then we'll go shopping."

"What about the sword?" Bagule asked.

"It can wait," Ephraim said. "First things, first. I doubt if anyone else is looking for it. As powerful as it is, no one in this world would be interested."

"There is one," Bagule said.

Ephraim's eyebrows rose. "There is? Interesting. I guess that means we need to hurry."

"Indeed," Nieleni replied.

"Follow me."

Ephraim led Bagule and Nieleni into the Heathrow parking garage. Ephraim's vehicle was much larger than those Bagule had encountered earlier. The djinn servant opened the rear door, gesturing for Bagule and Nieleni to enter. The leather covered seats were comfortable. Ephraim entered the front compartment then strapped in.

"Okay then, let's get this adventure started!" he said.

Ephraim steered the vehicle from the parking deck and into London traffic. The roads were as congested as they were in Lagos, but much more orderly. Marai was a big city, but it paled in comparison to cities such as London and Lagos. But where what Marai lacked in size, it made up for in spirit. The more time he spent away from the city, the more he appreciated Jakada's decision to keep the city separated from the rest of humanity. However, it was not his choice to make. He could also see how the citizens of Marai could be an example among these people. With their powers and his leadership, they could transform this world into something better, something beautiful.

Ephraim took them to London's market district. Ephraim parked his car, and Bagule and Nieleni followed him into a number of buildings that were markets within themselves. One of the buildings sold clothing. They entered and a merchant with extremely pale skin and red hair approached them.

"Welcome to Harrison's," the woman said. "How can I help you?"

"My friends need a wardrobe appropriate for the weather," Ephriam said.

"Splendid!" the woman said. "I'm Marissa. I'll be your wardrobe consultant."

The woman circled Nieleni, a wide grin on her face.

"You're quite lovely!" she said. "Have I seen you in *Vogue*?"

"What is Vogue?" Nieleni asked.

Marissa giggled. "You're kidding, right?"

Ephriam stepped in.

"Marissa, we haven't much time. My clients have a meeting to attend."

"Oh, I'm sorry," Marissa said. "Let's speed things up then. Javier!"

A short, brown-skinned man emerged from behind the checkout counter, wearing a tailor-made suit.

"Yes, Marissa?"

"Can you help this handsome man find a wardrobe while I work with this African goddess?"

"Of course! Can you follow me Mr. . . . ."

Bagule forced a smile on his face.

"Bagule."

"Okay, Mr. Bagule!" Javier said. "Follow me."

The consultants selected clothing for Bagule and Nieleni. Nieleni was not pleased with any of their selections, but to save time Bagule ordered her to choose from what they offered. Ephraim exchanged currency for the clothing; they left the market district then drove to their lodging.

The hotel was grand, taller and more spacious than the Sana's palace. Ephraim led them to check in where they secured their rooms.

"I'll be waiting for you in the lobby," he said. "Don't tarry. We have an afternoon appointment."

"With whom?" Nieleni asked.

"Someone who will be useful in our search for the sword."

Bagule and Nieleni entered the elevator together. Nieleni pressed the button to take them to their floor.

"I don't trust him," she said.

"You don't trust anyone," Bagule replied. "That is your duty."

He leaned toward her, then kissed her cheek.

"If it makes you feel better, I don't trust him either."

"At least he's human," she said. "If he betrays us, I can kill him."

"I don't think you'll have to, at least not until after we know where the sword is hidden. I'm sure he stands to receive much wealth if he delivers the sword to the Mansa."

"We need our own people. People we can trust," Nieleni said.

"There is no such thing as trust in this world," Bagule replied. "Loyalty belongs to the highest bidder. We must improve our position in that regard."

"What are you planning?" Nieleni asked.

"They use paper for money," Bagule said. "After our visit, I will increase our fortunes significantly."

Bagule raised his hand, then opened it. He closed his eyes and a pound sterling appeared. He smiled at Nieleni.

"It will be that simple."

CHAPTER FIFTEEN

Amber sat at the kitchen table, scarfing down a bowl of cereal. Summer had finally arrived. Never had she been so grateful to see the end of a school year. Her sophomore year had been a disaster. The good thing was the summer league was beginning and she would be on the soccer field again playing with people she actually liked. The best part was that she and Jasmine would be teammates again. As Jasmine would say, it wasn't fair to everyone else.

Mama burst into the kitchen, interrupting her peaceful grazing.

"They're here!" she shouted.

Amber put down her spoon, lifted the bowl to her mouth and drank the rest of her cereal and milk. She wiped her mouth with her napkin then followed Mama through the foyer and out the front door. A black SUV pulled into their driveway and Amber smiled. She hadn't seen Harriet since she was a little girl. The back door to the SUV swung open and a long-legged gangly girl with afro puffs and a huge grin on her face jumped out. Amber's eyes went wide.

"Harriet?" she said

"Amber!" Harriet exclaimed.

Harriet bounded toward Amber, her arms opened wide. Amber barely had time to open her arms before Harriet slammed into her. They fell into the grass together.

"It's so good to see you, Cuz!" Harriet said.

"Ow," Amber replied.

"Get off that girl, Harriet," Aunt Terry said.

Harriet scrambled off Amber then helped her sit up. They stared at each other for a second, then laughed.

"So, you got a little bigger," Amber said.

"Little, I'm a giant!" Harriet replied.

They stood and hugged properly this time. Aunt Terry walked over and gave Amber a hug.

"Hey, Amby," she said. "You've grown into a beautiful young lady."

"Thank you, auntie," Amber answered.

Amber looked over Aunt Terry's shoulder and saw Uncle Jesse stepping out of the car. He was the tallest man she knew. The sweetest, too.

"Come on over here and give your uncle a hug, baby girl!" he said.

Amber ran to him and hugged him.

"Hey unc!" she said. Amber smelled a familiar aroma.

"You're still smoking cigars," she said.

"Yes, I am," he replied.

"Terry, Jesse!"

Daddy came out the house with a big smile on his face.

"It's so good to see y'all!"

His eyes got wide when he saw Harriet.

"Is this Harriet? Little Harriet?"

"Hey Uncle!" Harriet said.

Daddy hugged Harriet while he looked at the others.

"Y'all come on inside. It's hot out here."

Everyone followed Daddy into the house. Amber let her senses free for a moment and reveled in the pleasant colors emanating from everyone. Mama and Aunt Terry hadn't spoken in years. Amber didn't know why they had a falling out, but the reasons diminished soon after Grandma announced she was staying in Africa. They formed a tag team trying to get Grandma to change her mind, and in the process became close again. Daddy and Uncle Jesse were close as well; both of them were former athletes and liked to try to out boast each other about their exploits. Amber's eyes fell to Harriet and she caught her breath. Harriet was looking at her strangely. A thought emerged in her head; *did she know?*

Uncle Jesse took Harriet's bags to the guest room, then hurried downstairs to gossip with the grownups. Amber grabbed Harriet's hand.

"Let's go to my room," she said.

Amber led her younger cousin to her room. As she entered the room, Harriet pulled her hand away. Amber spun around as she sat on the bed.

"What?" she said.

"Your room is so cool!" Harriet said.

"It's just a room," Amber replied.

"You don't remember, do you?" Harriet said. "You never used to let me in your room. You said I might break something."

"Get in here, girl," Amber said as she waved her hand.

Harriet skipped over to Amber's chair, scooping up the pillow that rested on the seat then hugged it as she sat.

"So, what have you been doing besides growing like a weed?" Amber asked.

"I run track!" Harriet answered. "I run the four by 400 and hurdles. And I'm fast like Mama and daddy. I bet I can beat you running now."

Amber laughed. "We'll see later. No soccer like your big cousin?"

Harriet sighed. "No. My feet get mixed up."

"Don't give up," Amber said. "I'll show you some stuff while you're here. You'll be coming to my games, too."

"Cool!"

Amber watched Harriet studying her room. Her eyes stopped at her mirror and lingered.

"So, do you have a boyfriend?"

The question broke Harriet's concentration. She jerked her head toward Amber, her eyes wide.

"NO!" she said.

Amber laughed. "You look guilty. Spill it."

"Well, there is this boy. His name is Jamal. He's really cute and he's the only boy in my class as tall as me."

"That'll change," Amber said. "The other boys will get taller. Maybe not cuter, but definitely taller."

Harriet's attention was drawn back to her mirror. Amber's suspicions increased.

"What's wrong?" she asked.

"I don't know," Harriet replied. "It seems . . ."

"What?"

"It looks like your mirror is moving."

A lump formed in Amber's throat. She opened up her senses. Harriet was a swirl of hues. She was definitely upset about her mirror.

"Harriet, can I ask you a question?"

"Ah, yeah," Harriet answered. Her eyes locked on the mirror.

"Have you been having any strange dreams lately?"

Harriet's hue turned deep purple. She was afraid.

"I always have strange dreams," she answered.

"Me too," Amber answered. "But has there been one particular one you keep having?"

Harriet swallowed. "Yes."

Amber took her hand.

"Tell me about it."

"Well . . ."

"Amber! Harriet! What are you girls doing up there?"

Amber rolled her eyes at the sound of Mama's voice. Her gesture lightened Harriet's mood. Her hue transformed into a bright blue as she giggled.

"The grownups demand our presence," Amber said. "We'll talk later."

Amber and Harriet went downstairs to join the rest of the family. They suffered the questions and teases then were forced to teach Mama and Aunt Terry the latest dances while Daddy lit the grill and barbequed. When the food was done, they sat under the patio canopy and ate while fanning away flies. Amber and Harriet finally had their race; Harriet pushed Amber hard but Amber prevailed. Harriet tackled her when she realized she wasn't going to win. They fell into the grass and laughed.

They came into the house from the heat and enjoyed ice cream and cake before Harriet's parents said their goodbyes and headed out. The girls helped Mama and Daddy clean up then lounged in the family room watching TV until almost midnight.

Amber was putting up her hair when Harriet peeked into her room.

"Amber, can we finish talking?"

Amber waved Harriet into her room.

"Close the door," she said.

Harriet closed the door, then sat on the edge of Amber's bed.

"It's this certain dream," she began. "I wouldn't be talking about it, but it seems so real. Sometimes when I wake up, I expect to be there."

"Where?" Amber asked.

"It's a city, an old city from ancient Africa," Harriet continued. "It looks like pictures of Timbuktu or Djenne, but it's not them."

"How do you know it's not them?" Amber asked.

"I just know," Harriet said. "I see myself walking down the streets. The people smile at me as I pass; some of them even bow. I feel so good there, better than I feel here. It's as if I belong there."

She looked at Amber, her eyes wide and innocent.

"Have you ever felt like that in a dream before?"

Amber hesitated before answering. Harriet had the gift, too. For some reason it had skipped a generation and been passed to them. The question now was should she tell Harriet what was happening to her, or should she take it even further and have Grandma reveal everything to her?

"My granddaughters are together at last."

Amber and Harriet looked toward her mirror where the voice had come from.

"Aaak!" Harriet squealed.

"Grandma?" Amber said.

Grandma's face coalesced in the mirror. Harriet scooted across the bed to Amber, then hugged her tight.

"Don't be afraid," Grandma said.

Amber hugged Harriet back.

"She's right," she said. "Don't be afraid."

Harriet looked up into Amber's face, surprise in her eyes.

"What's happening?" she asked.

"Something that's supposed to happen, I guess," Amber replied. "This has to do with the dreams you've been having."

"Who is that in the mirror?" Harriet asked.

"Grandma Corliss," Amber answered.

"But Grandma Corliss is old," Harriet said.

"Not anymore," Amber replied.

"Harriet?" Grandma said.

"It's okay," Amber said.

Harriet let go of Amber then looked toward the mirror.

"Is this really you, Grandma?" she said.

"It is," Grandma replied. "You've grown so much since the last time I saw you, Sprout."

Harriet turned to Amber, a bright smile creasing her face.

"It's her!" she said. "She called me Sprout!"

Harriet moved closer to the mirror.

"Where are you, Grandma?"

"I'm in the city you dreamed about," Grandma answered. "The city is called Marai, and it's my home."

Amber looked on as Grandma explained to Harriet what had happened to them. She knew exactly what Harriet was feeling; she'd experienced it herself only a few years ago. The memories of her adventure flashed through her mind and she felt every emotion. Sometimes it still didn't feel real.

The room fell silent for a moment. Harriet looked down, her face contemplative. When she looked at Amber and Grandma again, resolve ruled her expression.

"Why is this happening now?" she asked. "Is there something I must do?"

Grandma smiled. "You're very perceptive. As a matter of fact, there is a task for you."

Grandma's answer surprised Amber.

"Wait," she said. "You can't just pull Harriet into this."

"She's already involved," Grandma said. "There's a reason we cannot find the Sword of Sonni Ali. We weren't meant to. That is Harriet's duty."

"I don't understand," Amber said. "Harriet just got here. She just realized what's been happening to her."

"That's true. But Harriet has knowledge that will lead us to the sword."

"I do?" Harriet said.

"Yes, you do."

Grandma emerged from the mirror. Harriet jumped from the bed and ran across the room. Amber met her there.

"It's okay," she said. "This is how we travel."

"Through mirrors?" Harriet asked.

"Yes," Amber replied. "Just like that."

Harriet inched her way to Grandma. Once she reached her, a broad smile graced her face. She wrapped her arms around Grandma then pressed her cheek against her chest.

"Granny!" she said.

Grandma hugged Harriet and grinned.

"I always hated you calling me that, but I guess I'll have to get used to it."

Harriet sat on the bed, pulling Grandma with her. Amber sat beside her, reveling in the warm colors and emotions emanating from both of them.

"Tell me about Africa, Granny," Harriet said.

"Before I tell you about Africa, how about you tell me what you know about Songhai."

"Songhai is the empire that replaced Mali in the sixteenth century," she said. "It's first ruler, Sonni Ali was known as a great warrior and expanded the empire. When he died, Askia Mohammed became ruler after wresting power from Sonni Ali's son."

Grandma looked at Amber and Amber nodded back.

"What do you know about his sword?" Amber asked.

"Well, some people say it was enchanted," Harriet replied. "They say the reason Sonni Ali was powerful was because he was a sorcerer. They say he used his sword to command armies of djinn. But that's just hearsay."

"What do you think it looks like?" Grandma asked.

Harriet looked dumbfounded. "I don't know!"

Grandma smiled.

"Try to imagine it."

Harriet looked at Amber with worry.

"Go ahead," Amber said. "It's a game Grandma and I used to play all the time."

"Okay," Harriet said.

Harriet took a deep breath, then closed her eyes.

"I see a man," she began. "He's wearing some kind of uniform, French army, I think. He's in a mud mosque. By the look on his face, he's not supposed to be there. He's searching . . . he's searching for Sonni Ali's sword!"

Harriet's eyes opened wide.

"Was that real?" she asked. "Was I seeing into the past?"

"Yes," Grandma said. "You were."

"So, we know the sword was stolen by a French officer," Amber said. "That doesn't tell us where it is."

"But it gives us an idea," Grandma replied. "Harriet, I need you to go back again."

"I don't think I want to," Harriet said. "I've seen all those time travel stories. What if they can see me? I might change history and make things worse than they are now."

"That won't happen," Grandma said. "You are an observer, nothing more. What has happened cannot be altered. The past is the past."

"That sucks," Harriet said.

"I thought you didn't want to change anything," Amber said.

"I don't," Harriet replied. "But it would be cool if I could."

Amber rolled her eyes. "Girl, please."

"Let's focus," Grandma interjected. "Let's try this again, Harriet."

Harriet closed her eyes.

"I'm in France now. It's Paris; I can see the Eiffel Tower. I'm looking at the man who took the sword from the mosque. He's much older now and doesn't look well. There's a younger woman walking with him. I think it's his daughter. They're meeting with two men."

Harriet's eyebrows wrinkled and she grunted. Amber touched her shoulder.

"Are you okay?" she asked.

"I'm fine," Harriet replied. "I'm trying to hear what they're saying."

Amber looked to Grandma. "Can she do that?"

Grandma shrugged. "I don't know. I guess we'll find out."

"The old man is thanking the two men. They hand him a satchel and the woman gives them the box. One of the men tells the old man that the sword will be well taken care of. He has a British accent."

"So, the sword is in England?" Amber said.

"No," Harriet said. "There's more. I see a young woman with the sword case. She's on an ocean liner with lots of people. I see the Statue of Liberty!"

"The sword is in New York!" Amber exclaimed.

"It might be," Grandma said. "If the woman remained there."

Harriet opened her eyes.

"Wow, that was crazy!" Harriet said.

"Was there more?" Grandma asked.

"No, that was it," Harriet replied. "It was like I hit a wall or something."

"The sword is in New York," Grandma concluded. "We must go there immediately before Bagule discovers its whereabouts."

"Who is Bagule?" Harriet asked.

"A very dangerous man," Amber replied.

"Amber, contact Bissau," Grandma continued. "And we'll have to tell your mother, too."

"Who is Bissau?" Harriet asked. "And your mother knows about all this?"

"Bissau is a boy from Marai," Amber said. "He was sent here to protect and train me."

"Protect you? From what?" Harriet asked.

"I'll explain later," Amber said. "First, we need to talk to Mama."

"It's late," Grandma said. "We can wait until tomorrow. For now, you two get some rest. Tomorrow will be a busy day."

Harriet jumped from the bed and gave Grandma a hug.

"I missed you, Granny!" she said.

Grandma stroked her head. "I missed you too, Sprout."

Grandma looked up at Amber and their eyes met. She was always blue, radiating calm no matter what the situation.

"You're the teacher now," Grandma said.

Amber bit her lip. She was still learning, how was she going to teach Harriet?

"I'll do my best," Amber said.

"I know you will."

Harriet let go of Grandma and she stepped back through the shimmering mirror. Harriet faced Amber; her eyes wide.

"Oh, my goodness!" she said. "We're magical!"

She fell onto her back and kicked her feet. Amber laughed.

"Calm down, Harriet Potter," Amber said. "We need to get some sleep."

Harriet rolled over onto her stomach. "How am I supposed to sleep? Did you see what just happened? Did you see what I just did?"

Amber stood then ambled over to her dresser. She opened the top drawer and took out an old iPod with headphones. She gave it to Harriet.

"An iPod? This thing is ancient!"

"There's some good music on it," Amber said. "Now go back to your room and listen to it. It will help you sleep."

Harriet shrugged then stuck the earphones into her ears and turned on the iPod.

"Cool!"

Amber guided her to the door.

"See you in the morning."

Harriet waved. "See you!"

Amber watched Harriet line dance down the hall and into the guest room. She went back into the room, cut off the light and fell into her bed. Harriet was right. She wouldn't be able to sleep. She texted Bissau.

Hi Amber. It's late, What's going on?

I need you to come to my house tomorrow. Lots of things going on.

Like what?

My cousin is here. She's like me. She located the sword.

What time should I arrive?

Nine. My dad will be gone.

Oh my. I'll see you at nine.

Amber pushed the disconnect button on her phone then placed it on her nightstand. She hoped she would be able to sleep. Tomorrow would be an eventful day.

CHAPTER SIXTEEN

Stanton Castle nestled in the hills beyond London, a structural dinosaur from the days of wealthy nobility. Its current owners inherited the monstrosity from their parents, a the building sorely in need of repair. For years, they struggled to maintain the castle until the BBC approached the family to film a period piece show featuring the family home. The show was successful and the money flowed in. Now Stanton Castle was flush with pounds and visitors.

The people arriving during the rain on that morning had no interest in the castle's past or current fame. They were there for very different reasons. Bagule peered through the car window at the imposing building and frowned. His recent studies told him this castle and many others in this wet and wretched country were built from wealth stolen from throughout the world, particularly from the land now called Africa. Nieleni leaned from her side of the vehicle to gaze upon the structure as well. The expression on her face revealed she felt the same.

"Are you sure the sword is here?" Bagule asked Ephraim.

"No," Ephraim answered.

"Then why are we here?" Nieleni asked.

"I told you we were coming to meet someone who could tell us its whereabouts. It might be here, but it may not be."

"Then let's get on with it," Bagule said. "We're wasting time."

Bagule opened his door and stepped into the drizzle. Nieleni followed, opening her umbrella to cover them both. They waited on Ephraim, then walked to the front entrance of the castle. As they neared, they saw a sign on the door.

Closed for repairs.

"It's closed," Ephraim said. "We'll have to return tomorrow."

"Nonsense," Bagule said.

He nodded at Nieleni and she knocked on the door. There was no answer.

"Take my hand," Bagule said.

Nieleni took Bagule's hand.

"What are the owners' names?" he asked Ephraim.

"Byron and Elenore Kensington," Ephraim replied.

Bagule nodded then walked through the door, pulling Nieleni with him. Nieleni opened the door for Ephraim. The man entered, his eyes wide.

"I didn't know you could to that," he said.

"There's much you don't know about me," Bagule said.

"Excuse me, but how did you get in here?"

The trio turned to see a pale smartly-dressed middle-aged man staring at them. Bagule smiled, approaching the man with his hand extended.

"The door was open," Bagule said.

The man ignored the gesture. "Didn't you see the sign?" We're closed for repairs."

"Our apologies, Lord Kensington," Ephraim said. "The tour company apparently gave us the wrong information. I'm Ephraim Cole of Imperial Tours. These are my guests. They have come a long way to see your beautiful home."

Ephraim and Kensington shook hands.

"You can call me Byron," the man said. "We dropped such formalities a long time ago."

He turned his attention to Bagule and Nieleni.

"And who might I ask are you?"

Bagule reached out and took Nieleni's hand.

"I am Bagule Jawara," Bagule said. "This is my wife, Nieleni. We have traveled all the way from Mali to see your home. Are you familiar with Mali?"

"I can't say I am," Byron replied. "Somewhere in Africa, isn't it?"

"Yes," Nieleni replied curtly.

Byron took her hand and bowed slightly.

"Welcome," Byron said. "That television show has been a blessing and a curse. In your case, I consider it a blessing."

"We don't wish to bother you," Bagule said. "But since we're here, would you mind giving us a brief tour?"

"Not at all," Byron said. "Be glad that Elenore isn't here. She's very strict about visiting hours. She enjoys her privacy."

"And where is the lady of the house?" Nieleni asked.

"Away visiting relatives while the renovations are being completed," Byron said. "She hates the noise and the dust."

Bagule, Nieleni and Ephraim shared smiles.

"Please, follow me," Byron said.

They followed Lord Kensington as he described the various objects of the castle. Bagule barely listened. He studied every room with his eyes and senses, seeking the sword. Although there were many antique objects from around the world, they had yet to come across the sword.

"This is very interesting Byron," Bagule finally said. "However, there is one item I would like to ask you about."

Byron turned to Bagule.

"What is it?"

"There is a relic of great value that used to reside in an old mosque in Timbuktu. It was a sword. Some say it's the sword of the Songhai emperor, Sonni Ali."

Byron rubbed his chin. "I don't know what you're talking about."

"The sword was taken from the mosque by a French officer during the nineteenth century. The stories say it was sold to someone in your family upon the Frenchman's death," Ephraim said.

Byron frowned as he rolled his eyes.

"You aren't some of those reclamation people, are you?" he asked. "I thought we were rid of you people."

Nieleni stepped toward Byron.

"You people?"

Byron stepped away, raising his hands.

"I didn't mean it that way," he said. "We recently returned any artifacts our ancestors had acquired from countries around the world."

"He's lying," Nieleni said.

She sprang, grabbing Byron by the throat, then pushing him into the nearest chair.

"Where is the sword?" she said.

Byron's eyes were wide with fear. Bagule stood beside Nieleni, a smile on his face.

"This isn't necessary," Ephraim said.

"Be quiet," Bagule retorted. He turned his attention back to Byron.

"As you can see, my wife has lost her patience," he said. "Now give us the sword and we'll be on our way."

"I don't have it!" Byron said.

"You're still lying," Nieleni replied. She increased the pressure on his neck.

"It's gone!" Byron managed to say.

"Gone where?" Bagule asked.

"It's true that my family purchased the sword from the Frenchman. But my great-great grandmother took it to America. She had a falling out with the family and fled to the states."

"Where?" Bagule asked.

"I don't know," Byron said. "The family disowned her soon afterward. We think she went to New York, but we weren't certain. As far as the others were concerned, she was dead."

Nieleni glanced at Bagule, the sorcerer nodded, and she released him.

"He knows nothing," Bagule said.

Byron rubbed his bruised throat.

"You think you'll get way with this?" he said. "I'm alerting the authorities. I'll have you deported!"

Bagule grinned. "How can you share what you don't remember?"

Bagule touched Byron's forehead. The man blinked a few times, a bewildered look on his face. He finally focused on the trio then jumped to his feet.

"Who are you?" he said. "And what are you doing here? We're closed for repairs."

"We apologize," Bagule said. "We came a long way to visit your castle. We saw the sign, but since the door was open, we let ourselves in."

Ephraim stepped in. "We apologize for the intrusion. We'll leave immediately."

The trio walked toward the door.

"I don't suppose you would like a tour, seeing as though you're already inside," Byron said.

"No thank you," Nieleni replied. "We have what we came for."

"Pardon me?" Byron asked.

"Have a good day, Lord Kensington," Bagule said.

The left the castle then strode through the rain back to the car.

"The sword is in New York," Bagule said. "What is this New York?"

"It's a city in America," Ephraim said. "You'll need help, lots of help."

"Can you arrange it?" Nieleni asked.

"Yes, I can," Ephraim replied.

Bagule grinned.

"Then we travel to New York," he said.

CHAPTER SEVENTEEN

Amber awoke to the day full of anxious anticipation. No sooner had she sat up in her bed did she hear tapping at her door.

"Amber? Are you awake?"

"Yeah," she called out.

Harriet opened the door and stuck her head inside, a nervous smile on her face. Amber waved her in, and she came inside, then fell on her bed.

"Did you sleep?" Amber asked.

"Nope," Harriet replied. "How could I? I found out last night that I'm a wizard!"

Amber rolled her eyes. "You're not a wizard."

"Then what do you call it?" Harriet asked. "A sorcerer, a witch?"

"I don't know," Amber said. "I never asked."

The smell of sausage wafted into the room and Amber was suddenly hungry.

"Mama's starting breakfast," she said. "Let's go help her."

The girls put on their robes then made their way to the kitchen. Mama was over the stove, stirring the grits while sausage sizzled in the iron skillet. She looked up to see the girls and a bright smile filled her face.

"Well hello, ladies," she said. "I didn't expect you two up so early. I figured you stayed up all night talking about boys."

"Boys? Ugh!" Harriet said.

"No need to put up a front, Miss Harriet," Mama said. "Your mother already told me about your crush. What's his name?"

Harriet pulled out a chair and sat down hard.

"I hate her!"

"No, you don't," Mama said. "We're sisters. We don't have secrets."

"We came to help with breakfast," Amber said. "What can we do?"

"You can go upstairs and tell you daddy breakfast is almost ready," Mama replied.

"Okay," Amber said.

"And you stop being mad at your Mama," Amber's mother said to Harriet. "She couldn't help it. I'm nosey."

Amber hurried upstairs, then knocked on the door.

"Is breakfast ready, Amber?" Daddy asked.

"How did you know it was me?" she asked.

"Your Mama never knocks," Daddy said. "I could be in here butt naked and she'll just barge right in."

"Eww," Amber said. "Maybe you should lock the door."

Daddy came out of the room dressed for work. He hugged Amber, lifting her off her feet. She smiled, then hugged him back.

"You leave me any sausage?" he asked.

"It's not done yet," she answered. "If it was, it would all be gone."

"My greedy daughter," he said as they walked down the stairs together.

"I'm a growing girl," she said.

"I wish my paycheck was, too," Daddy replied.

Harriet and Mama were eating when daddy and Amber entered the kitchen. Amber let daddy make his plate first, that way she would have free rein over anything left. Daddy winked at her as he piled his plate with sausage.

"Hey! That's not fair!" she fussed.

"If I don't eat them all, I'll put them back," Daddy said. "I know better."

Daddy sat at the table while Amber made her plate. The four of them enjoyed a leisurely breakfast, Mama and Daddy teasing each other as Amber and Harriet laughed. The mood helped ease the tension Amber felt inside.

After breakfast, Amber and Harriet washed the dishes as Mama walked Daddy to the door and kissed him goodbye. She was about to go upstairs to prepare for work when Amber called out.

"Mama, can we talk for a minute?" she said.

Mama entered the kitchen then sat at the table.

"What is it, Baby?"

Amber nodded at Harriet. They dried their hands and sat with Mama.

"Mama, Harriet is like me," Amber said.

"Like you? What do you mean . . ."?

Mama's eyes went wide and she covered her mouth. Amber nodded.

"Yes. She's got powers. Grandma visited us last night and confirmed it."

"Mama was here? Why didn't you tell me?"

"She was here for a reason," Amber said.

"What reason?"

"We need to go to New York," Amber said.

Mama dropped her head into in her hands.

"Oh, my lord," she said. "Why did you have to tell me this before work?"

"Grandma told me to tell you first thing in the morning," Amber replied. "She said we had to get started as soon as we could or we won't get the sword."

Mama jerked up her head. "Sword? What sword? What's going on, Amber?"

"I better let Grandma explain," Amber said.

Amber grabbed Mama's hand and led her to her room. She opened her top drawer, then took out a bag of dust.

"What is that?" Mama asked.

"It's how I communicate with Grandma," Amber answered.

She took a pinch of dust, then blew it into the mirror. The glass shimmered, swirled, then revealed the interior of Grandma's room. Grandma sat on a low stool with her back turned to them as she combed her hair.

"Grandma?" Amber said.

Grandma turned to them, then grinned.

"You're all here," she said. "Good."

Mama moved Amber out of the way.

"Hey, Mama!" she said.

"Hey, Baby," Grandma replied.

Mama pressed her hand to the mirror glass; Grandma did the same and they shared a smile.

"I can feel your warmth," Mama said.

"I feel yours, too," Grandma replied.

"I'm still not used to seeing you like this," Mama said. "I think you're younger than me now!"

"Only in appearance," Grandma said.

"I told Mama about New York and the sword," Amber said.

Grandma nodded. "We must get the girls and Bissau there immediately before Bagule discovers where the sword is and claims it."

"What a minute," Mama said. "Bissau? That cute boy Amber likes? What does he have to do with this?"

"I don't like him!" Amber said. "Mama, Bissau is from Marai. He was sent here to watch over me and train me."

"Oh Lord!" Mama sat down. "This too much!"

"Can you get the children to New York?" Grandma asked.

Mama shook her head. "Not this quickly. I have to make arrangements. I have to book a hotel, buy tickets, and explain to your father why we're all of a sudden flying to New York for no good reason!"

Grandma looked pensive before she spoke.

"Then we have no choice," she finally said. "We'll have to use the mirrors."

The doorbell rang.

"That's probably Bissau," Amber said. "We'll be back in a minute, Grandma."

"No 'we' won't," Mama said. "That boy is not coming up to your room . . .unless he's been up here already!"

Amber rolled her eyes. "No, he hasn't, Mama. I told you I don't like him like that!"

"She's not like you were," Grandma said.

"Be quiet, Mama!"

Amber hurried downstairs, Mama and Harriet close behind. She peeked through the glass window bordering the front door. Bissau saw her and waved. Amber unlocked the door and opened it. Bissau's eyes went wide.

"Ah, hello Mrs. Robinson," he said. "How are you?"

"I've been better," Mama replied. "So, you're magic, too?"

Bissau looked at Amber and sighed. "Yes, ma'am."

"Bissau, Harriet found the sword," Amber said.

Bissau stepped into the house.

"Where is it?"

"New York," Amber replied. "We have to go today. We must travel through the mirrors."

Bissau's face took on a serious countenance.

"I'm ready," he said.

"What does he mean, 'he's ready?'" Mama asked.

"Bissau's specialty is mirror jumping," Amber explained. "He will go ahead to make sure our path is safe."

"He's a boy!" Mama exclaimed.

"Where I come from, I have been a man for two years," Bissau said.

"He's very mature for his age," Amber added.

Mama spun about then marched upstairs.

"I can't," she said. "I'm going to work. Y'all figure this out. Whatever y'all do, be back before I get home."

"Let's go to my room," Amber said. "Grandma is waiting."

Harriet leaned toward Amber, then whispered in her ear.

"He's cute," she said.

"Not now, Harriet," Amber replied outloud.

Amber led everyone to her room where Grandma waited.

"Where's Cheryl?" Grandma asked.

"She's gone to work," Amber said. "She said whatever we did, we need to be back before dinner."

Grandma shook her head before gazing at Bissau.

"Hello, Warrior," she said.

Bissau bowed. "Hello, Alake. How may I serve you?"

"You're a warrior?" Harriet asked.

Bissau turned and smiled at Harriet.

"Yes."

"Cool!" Harriet exclaimed.

"You must find us a safe path," Grandma said.

"I will," Bissau replied.

"Be safe."

Grandma's image faded.

"Harriet, we need you to touch the mirror and imagine where you think the sword may be," Bissau said.

"I tried to find it before, but I couldn't," Harriet replied.

"That's okay," Amber said. "Get us as close as you can."

"Okay."

Harriet stepped to the mirror, placed her palm against it then closed her eyes. The mirror began shifting and she jerked her hand away."

"What's wrong?" Amber asked her.

"It felt weird," she replied.

"It usually does the first time," Bissau said. "Come, let's do it together."

Bissau grasped Harriet's hand and she giggled.

"Oh boy," Amber said.

Bissau placed Harriet's hand on the mirror, then put his hand beside hers.

"Try again," he said.

Harriet closed her eyes. The mirror surface swirled for a moment until the interior of a room appeared. Bissau closed his eyes, then opened them. He took Harriet's hand away from the mirror. The image remained.

He smiled at Amber and Harriet.

"I'll be back," he said.

Bissau jumped into the mirror and the image disappeared. Harriet stumbled away.

"He jumped into the mirror!" she said.

"Yes, that's what he did," Amber replied.

"So, what to do we do now?" Harriet asked.

Amber sat down and pulled Harriet down beside her.

"The only thing we can do. We wait."

CHAPTER EIGHTEEN

Bissau tumbled through the void in confusion. It had been some time since he'd traveled, and he'd lost some of his skills. It took him a moment to adjust and focus on his destination. Moments later, he emerged from the mirror, the sound of glass shattering preceding him. He hit the floor hard on his chest, the air forced from his lungs. As he gasped for breath, he looked at his hands. They were bleeding.

"Someone's in the room!" he heard a man's voice shout.

Bissau panted as he clambered to his feet. The room was almost completely dark except for a faint illumination radiating from a nearby pedestal. On top of the pedestal was a curved sword inside of a scabbard decorated with gold and jewels.

"Sonni Ali's sword!" Bissau whispered.

He searched the room as heavy footfalls became louder. There was another mirror; he could grab the sword then leap through. There was a risk; he had no time to find out where the mirror would take him. He ran to the sword, reaching for the case and was blown back by an invisible force. Bissau slid across the floor, then struck the opposite wall.

Through his pain, he heard the people outside struggling to open the door. Bissau climbed to his feet, then sprinted for the other mirror. He pulled the dust pouch from his pocket, sprinkled the contents onto his left palm then blew. He was leaping through when the door opened.

"There he . . ."

Bissau fell through the mirror. This time he was prepared. He landed on his feet, his hands raised to defend himself. He was lucky again; the room was empty. He took his time blowing the dust onto the mirror, then placed his palms against it. Bissau shifted through the images appearing before him until he saw Amber and Harriet staring at him. He lowered his hands, then stepped through the glass. He emerged in Amber's room.

Amber smiled until she saw his bleeding hands.

"Oh my god!" she exclaimed. "What happened?"

"The mirror on the other side broke as I passed through," he said. "That's never happened before."

Amber grabbed his wrist.

"Come with me."

She led Bissau into her bathroom.

"Sit," she said.

Bissau sat at her vanity chair. Amber went into her cabinet and took out alcohol, swabs, and antibiotic. She soaked the swab with alcohol, then began wiping his palms.

"Did you find the sword?" she asked.

"Yes," Bissau replied. "But I wasn't there long enough to figure out exactly where I was. It's being protected."

Amber stopped cleaning his wounds. "Protected?"

"Yes," Bissau said. "They knew as soon as I entered the room. I tried to take the sword, but some force repelled me. By the time I recovered, the others were entering the room. I had to flee, so I jumped through another mirror in the room. From there, I came here."

Amber applied antibiotic to his wounds. "So, they know we can travel through the mirrors. They will remove them from the room and increase security. We'll have to find another way in."

"How about through the door?" Harriet said.

Amber sighed. "I wish it was that simple."

"Maybe it is," Harriet said.

Harriet approached them, holding up her cellphone.

"I found this."

It was an image of a brownstone building nestled on a nondescript street. A sign hung from the awning.

"It's the Museum of African Artifacts in Harlem," she said. "Not too many people know about it. I'll bet the sword is here."

"It may be," Bissau said. "But whoever possesses the sword doesn't want it known that they have it. The room was sealed, and the sword was protected by nyama. They know of its power."

Amber placed cotton pads on Bissau's hands, then wrapped them in gauze.

"Isn't this a bit much?" he asked.

Amber frowned. "You're welcome."

"Thank you," Bissau said, looking a little embarrassed.

"We have to go to New York today," Amber said.

"I'll have to find another mirror for us," Bissau said.

"No, we have to fly," Amber replied. "We might have to stay a few days."

"But Auntie said we can't," Harriet chimed in. "It would take too long to plan."

Amber was quiet for a moment. "We have to go without her."

"We can't do that!" Harriet said.

"You don't have to go," Amber said. "It's Bissau and my responsibility."

"But you won't be able to find where the sword is without me," Harriet replied.

Amber looked at Bissau.

"She's right," Bissau said.

"Where are we going to get the money?" Harriet asked. "Who's going to make the hotel reservations?"

"I have money," Bissau said.

"And I'll make the reservations," Amber added.

"This isn't smart," Harriet said. "We're going to get in so much trouble!"

"You have no idea what Bagule is capable of," Bissau said. "What he's planning to do will change my world and yours, and not in a good way."

The room was quiet for a moment before Amber spoke.

"Bissau, do you have your cards?"

Bissau took out his wallet. "Yes."

Amber took a deep breath. "Okay then. Let's do this."

CHAPTER NINETEEN

Bagule, Nieleni, and Ephraim exited the 727 into LaGuardia terminal. Bagule gazed about the crowded airport, a look of disdain on his face. Every new city he visited in the outside world solidified in his mind that what he was doing was right. This world was crowded, filthy, and corrupt. With the power he would possess once they gained the Sword, he would set things right not only for Marai, but for the world beyond Wagadu.

Wagadu. The prophesy had been on his mind much lately. When he found himself outside Marai's walls despair overtook him. In the first few moments, he thought death would be a better alternative than living outside the city. But as he and Nieleni struggled to survive, he realized that their exile from Marai was necessary. He had to see for himself what the world had become without the guidance of the Ancestors. It was then he realized his purpose went far beyond freeing the citizens of the city.

Ephraim made arrangements for them as he did in London. An Uber picked them up curbside then took them to their hotel in Manhattan. Ephraim spared no expense in their accommodations, booking a penthouse on the upper level of the hotel. Bagule was not impressed; he preferred to be closer to the ground. But there were items much more important than the elevation of a hotel room.

The trio gathered in the sitting area around the oval coffee table.

"The sword is here, and we are here," Bagule said. "Where do we begin?"

"The sword is probably in a museum," Ephraim said. "At least if we're lucky."

"What do you mean, lucky?" Nieleni asked.

"It's possible that whoever purchased it is keeping it in a private collection."

"How possible?" Bagule asked.

"I don't know," Ephraim replied. "Our best bet is to begin with the public museums as we research the private collections."

"Are there djinn in New York who can help us?" Bagule asked.

Ephraim sighed. "Yes, there are djinn here, but they will not help us."

"Why not?" Nieleni asked. She stood before the glass wall, staring at the buildings. "Don't they all answer to their Mansa?"

"Things are a bit more complex here," Ephraim said. "Djinn are no better than humans when it comes to power and influence. The djinn that came to these shores are exiles, those who defied the Mansa for various reasons. They are loosely organized and loyal to no one. This is probably why none of them have used it to their own advantage. Unless . . ."

"What?" Bagule asked.

Nieleni returned to the couch.

"Unless one of them did find it, and is keeping it for their own purposes," Ephraim finished.

"It would also mean that this djinn might be open to an alliance," Bagule said.

"It's possible, but we must be ready to deal with it if the situation becomes hostile," Nieleni said.

"I agree," Bagule said.

Ephraim was silent. He stared into his glass as he swirled the contents.

"Is there something bothering you, Ephraim?" Bagule asked.

"I have traveled here to help you find the Sword," he answered. "I'm not sure how I feel about fighting djinn."

"Then you are no longer any use to us," Nieleni said. "You should leave."

"Wait," Bagule said. He moved closer to Ephraim. "I understand how you feel. But didn't you just say that these djinn do not show loyalty to their Mansa?"

"Yes, I did say that," Ephraim replied.

Bagule cut his eyes at Nieleni. Nieleni smiled, then turned away.

"The Sword of Sonni Ali is a powerful talisman," Bagule began. "Anyone who obtains it and returns it to the Mansa should expect a handsome reward, don't you think?"

Ephraim nodded.

Bagule leaned closer to Ephraim. "Imagine when we return with the Sword and I share with the Mansa that nothing would have been possible without your help."

Ephraim grinned. "I can imagine it, because it would be true."

"Do you think your loyalty to djinn you barely know would be worth giving up such platitudes?"

Ephraim sat down his glass then looked directly into Bagule's eyes.

"No," he said.

"Good. Then let's stop wasting time. We have a djinn to find."

* * *

The subway ride to the Harlem district was cramped and uncomfortable. Bagule frowned at the woman leaning against him, but resisted the urge to shove her away. Ephraim briefed them on the etiquette of mass transit, which did not sit well with either of them. Nieleni was in a much worse state. The man who chose to sit by her talked constantly in an accent that made him hard to understand. Unlike him, Nieleni didn't hide her disdain, but it didn't deter the scruffy man. He continued to talk to her even as they reached their stop and exited the train. It was then she had her fill of him. She spun around then shoved the man to the ground. She was raising her right foot to step on his throat when Ephraim grabbed her arm and pulled her away. Nieleni snatched her arm free of Ephraim's grip, then raised her hand to strike him.

"No, Nieleni," Bagule said.

"He touched me," Nieleni replied.

Bagule walked to her, then grasped her hands.

"No, love," he said. "He is not our enemy. At least not yet."

Nieleni lowered her hands. Bagule turned to Ephraim, then nodded.

"Follow me," Ephraim said to them both.

They merged into the drably dressed throng, they walked up the stairs then out into Harlem. The streets bustled with brown-skinned people going about their way, a sight that was somewhat calming to Bagule.

"I see them," Ephraim said. "There are many here."

"Any nearby?" Bagule said.

"Yes, but they are avoiding me and each other," Ephraim replied. "It is very strange."

"Point one out to me," Nieleni asked.

Ephraim nodded his head toward a stout woman entering a nearby shop. Nieleni walked briskly to the shop, Bagule and Ephraim close behind. She turned to look at them both.

"Stay here," she said. "I'll be back."

Bagule and Ephraim had to wait only a few minutes when Nieleni emerged from the store with the woman, her hand gripped tightly around the woman's throat. The woman looked at Bagule with curiosity; her eyes fell on Ephraim and she grimaced.

"What are you doing here?" she asked with venom in her voice.

"We will ask the questions," Nieleni said.

The woman broke away from Nieleni with surprising strength.

"You really think you could hold me against my will? You foolish human! I only came to see this piece of camel dung that led you to me so I could spit in his face!"

The djinn's cheeks swelled as she attempted make good on her words. Bagule raised his hand.

"Stop," he said.

The djinn's eyes widened as her cheeks locked in place. Bagule walked up to her.

"I am Bagule, High Sorcerer of Marai. This is Nieleni, my companion, and this is Ephraim, our guide. Before I release you, you will promise me you will cooperate with us and answer all our questions honestly. Do you understand?"

The woman nodded. Bagule waved his hand and her cheeks deflated.

"Good," he said. "Now let's start again. What is your name?"

"Shakira Jones," she said.

"No, what is your djinn name?" Ephraim asked.

"We no longer keep the old traditions," Shakira answered. "I have only one name."

"That explains your weakness," Ephraim said.

Shakira's eyes narrowed. "I see I'm not the only weak one. You serve humans."

"I do so of my own free will," Ephraim said.

"Enough of this," Bagule said. "Solve your squabbles later. Shakira, we are here to find the djinn who possesses Sonni Ali's sword."

Bagule's words made Shakira grimace.

"I don't know who would want to possess such a thing," she said.

"Don't you?" Ephraim asked. "There must be at least one djinn who would aspire to such decadence, especially here."

Shakira's hand was swift. She slapped Ephraim so hard he stumbled backwards toward the street. Nieleni caught him as she chuckled.

"Stop this!" Bagule said. "Come, let us go somewhere we can talk."

"There's no need for that," Shakira said. "If there is any djinn foolish and pompous enough to go after Sonni Ali's sword, it would be Bahari Cole."

"Where can we find her?" Nieleni asked.

"She owns a brownstone mansion in central Harlem. It's not far from here."

Bagule stroked his chin. "Can you take us there?"

"I can show you the way," Shakira said. "I won't go near that place, nor will any other djinn and most humans. And don't be confident of your little tricks, Sorcerer. Bahari is a powerful djinn. Some say she rivals the Mansa."

"How do you know?" Ephraim said, still rubbing his jaw. "You have no idea how powerful she is."

"It is what some say," Shakira replied. "I could care less either way. Can I go now?"

"Tell us how to get to Bakari's mansion," Nieleni said.

Bagule felt a sharp pain in his head. Seconds later, the directions to the mansion formed in his mind. He looked at Shakira and she smirked.

"Things aren't always what they seem," she said. "Good luck on your quest. I hope you all die."

Shakira grabbed her bags, then hurried away. Nieleni started after her, but Bagule waved her still.

"We have what we need," he said. "Time for us to pay Bahari Cole a visit."

CHAPTER TWENTY

Bissau loaded Amber's bags into the trunk of the rideshare. Amber watched him, her hands trembling. They were actually doing this, going to New York without anyone's permission. Bissau turned to her, then smiled.

"It's okay, Amber," he said. "We'll be back in a few days."

"I'm breaking every rule known to kids," she said. "My parents will be furious."

"It's the price you must pay to save Marai," Bissau said. "Once you explain everything to them, they'll understand."

"That's easy for you to say," Amber said. "You have no one to answer to."

"I answer to Master Jakada," Bissau said. "And that is why I must do this."

They were interrupted by Harriet's arrival. She held her backpack and suitcase in her hands. Her entire body shook as she handed Bissau her luggage.

"You don't have to go," Amber said. "You can stay here and tell Mama and Daddy what's going on."

"I'm not sure I know what's going on," Harriet answered. "But I don't want to be here by myself. I'm going with y'all."

"Okay. I guess we're all in," Amber said.

They climbed into the car and were on their way. The driver drove them to Hartsfield/Jackson Airport, dropping them off at the Delta domestic flights terminal. Amber checked everyone in online, so they moved briskly through check in and security. The closer they came to the gate; the more nervous Amber became. She took Harriet's hand. Harriet looked at her, seeming relieved that she did.

"It's going to be okay," Amber said.

"Is it really?" Harriet asked.

Amber's smile faded. "Honestly, I don't know. But no matter what happens, Bissau and I will make sure nothing happens to you, okay?"

Harriet squeezed her hand. "Okay."

They boarded the airport shuttle to their gate, exiting moments later at their concourse. Amber led the way up the escalator and to their gate, distracting herself by window shopping along the way. They found three seats together and settled in. Harriet immediately plugged in her phone and donned her earplugs. Amber was about to do the same when she glanced at Bissau. He sat with his eyes closed as if asleep. She tapped him on his shoulder; he opened his eyes and smiled. Amber was reminded how pretty his eyes were.

"Are you okay?" she asked.

"I'm okay, Amber. How are you?"

"I'm nervous," she admitted.

"I understand," Bissau replied.

"How do you do it?" she asked.

"Do what?"

"Remain so calm," she said.

"I was trained for this," Bissau said. "Master Jakada told me that one day I would have to defend Marai and its people. For years I waited for the opportunity to do so. Now I'm here with you and Harriet."

"You're not a least bit nervous?"

"I am," he said. "Which is why I meditate. I remember my training, and I mentally go through all the situations that I've encountered in the past and how I've survived them."

"And that helps?"

Bissau smiled. "Sometimes. It reminds me of how so much of what we do is out of our control. We can only trust the ancestors."

"Trust the ancestors," Amber repeated.

Their boarding was announced. Bissau spared no expense for the journey, purchasing first class tickets for the three of them. The looks on the flight attendants' faces revealed their surprise, but they were pleasant and attentive. Twenty minutes later, they were airborne, on their way to New York City. There was no turning back. Amber and Harriet sat together, Bissau's seat was across the aisle from Amber. He leaned back in his seat with eyes closed, continuing his meditation. Amber glanced at Harriet; she had her earplugs in, still holding Amber's hand. Amber decided to try Bissau's method. She closed her eyes and let her mind drift back to when she was normal.

But the fact was she was never normal. She remembered when Grandma told her the stories of Marai at bedtime and she realized when she envisioned them, they were real to her. She shifted through her memories, seeing those days as her younger self told people what they were feeling and how they resented her for it. Her powers were making themselves known all along, but she was too young to understand and too afraid to tell anyone else. It wasn't until the incident in the bathroom after that fateful soccer game that she reached the point that she had to say something.

She'd been through so much since that day, adventures that took her to places she'd never imagined. Through it all she used her wits, her powers and most of all, her friends and family to make it through. A smile came to her face; no matter what they had to deal with, they would do it together. She understood now where Bissau gained his confidence.

The flight attendant announced their initial approach to La Guardia. Amber opened her eyes, then looked to Harriet. Her cousin was asleep and snoring. Amber squeezed her hand.

"Harriet?"

Harriet jerked up; her eyes wide. She looked at Amber as if she didn't know who she was.

"Huh? What? Oh, hey Amber!" she said. "I forgot where we were."

She raised up in her seat to look around the cabin.

"We're actually doing this," she said.

Amber nodded. "Yes, we are."

Amber felt a touch on her arm then turned to see Bissau smiling at her.

"Are you ready?" he asked.

Amber smiled back. "I am."

The seatbelt sign turned off and they exited the plane. Bissau contacted an Uber from his app; the driver waited for them as they exited the terminal with their bags. Their destination was an Airbnb nestled between Harlem and Manhattan. They would have the entire home to themselves.

The driver pulled up to the door. They took out their bags then sat them on the sidewalk as they stared at the entrance to the brownstone they'd rented.

"It looks old," Amber said.

"It is," Bissau replied. "I hope the mirrors are old as well. They make the best conduits."

"It looks haunted," Harriet added.

"It might be," Bissau said. "The presence of spirits is always welcomed."

"Did he just say ghosts are okay?" Harriet asked.

"Yes, I did," Bissau answered. "They are harmless, mostly."

Bissau picked up his bags, then went to the entrance. He unlocked the finely carved door then went inside.

"You first," Harriet said.

Amber took her hand. "How about we go in at the same time?"

Harriet nodded. Together, they squeezed through the door. The home was immaculately furnished, whether antiques or replicas Amber couldn't tell. Harriet let go of her hand and searched through the house.

"Bissau? Where are you?"

"Upstairs!" Bissau called out.

Amber closed and locked the front door, then led Harriet upstairs. The stairs ended at an open atrium with a stained glass skylight. Three bedrooms opened into the space.

"I'm in the middle room," Bissau said.

They entered the room and were greeted by Bissau's wide smile. He stood before a floor mirror edged by a simple frame.

"This is perfect!" he said. "I saw it in the pictures, but it is much more impressive standing in front of it."

"It's kind of plain," Harriet said.

"You're looking with the wrong eyes," Bissau said. "Touch it."

Amber and Harriet approached it with their right hands outstretched. They both jumped when they were a foot away and drew back their hands. The tingling sensation Amber felt traveled through her body then dissipated when it reached her feet.

"Oh wow!" she said.

"Yeah, wow!" Harriet echoed.

"I'm sure we'll be able to find the sword with this," Bissau said. "Come, let's begin."

"Hold up," Amber said. "I'm hungry."

"Me, too," Harriet agreed.

Bissau looked astonished. "How can you think of food now?"

"Like this."

Amber took out her phone and began searching for best Chinese restaurants in New York.

"Harriet, do you like Chinese food?" she asked.

"I do!" Harriet replied.

Amber looked at Bissau.

"How about you?"

"Are you serious?" Bissau said. "Are you really going to order Chinese food right now?"

Amber lowered her phone as she placed her hand on her hip.

"Look, if we touch that mirror and see the sword, then we'll have to go after it. Once that begins, we don't know what will happen. Whatever does, I don't want to be hungry, too."

"Yeah," Harriet said. "It's like our last meal."

Amber stared at Harriet. "Not exactly, Miss Morbid."

She turned her attention back to Bissau.

"So, I'll ask you again, do you like Chinese food?"

Bissau lowered his head in resignation.

"Yes."

Amber smiled. "See, that wasn't so hard!"

She walked to Bissau, then kissed him on the cheek. Bissau jerked his head up, surprise on his face.

"Wha . . .What was that for?"

"For making the arrangements to get us here," Amber said, although she wasn't sure that was the only reason.

"Can I order anything I want?" Harriet asked.

"Yep," Amber replied. "It's on me."

"Cool! I want shrimp fried rice with Mongolian Beef, chicken egg rolls and pot stickers!"

"Wow, that's a lot," Amber said. "What about you, Bissau?"

"Sweet and Sour chicken with fried rice," he said.

"Great. I'll get what Harriet's getting, with extra egg rolls."

Bissau shook his head.

"Both of you are bottomless pits," he said.

"Thank you," Amber replied.

Amber called in a delivery order while Bissau and Harriet took their things to their rooms. She took her bags to her room, then walked about the brownstone. There was something calming about it, as if they were meant to be there. She was downstairs in the kitchen when Bissau and Harriet joined her.

"Look!" Harriet said. "They left us cookies!"

On the table was a covered plate with an assortment of fresh baked cookies.

"I thought I recognized that smell," Amber said.

Harriet rushed to the table and began lifting the lid.

"Not yet," Amber said. "Let's eat dinner first."

Harriet turned and glared at Amber

"You're not my mom!" she said. She stuck her tongue, took a chocolate chip cookie from the plate, then ate it. Amber laughed.

"Children."

Amber and Bissau joined her. They had finished half the cookies when the doorbell rang. Bissau went to answer, returning a few minutes later loaded with Chinese food. Amber realized how hungry she was when the aromas hit her nose.

They took the food into the sitting room, eating while they channel surfed. Despite their relaxed attitude, Amber could see the tension. Bissau radiated a slight red hue while Harriet blazed orange with worry. She moved closer to her cousin and teased her as they ate until she saw her colors diminish. As they finished the last of the food, Bissau stood.

"It's time."

Harriet's colors flared to orange again. Amber put her arm around her.

"Come on," she said. "The sooner we do it, the sooner it's over. We can be back home as soon as tomorrow."

The three of them climbed the stairs, then entered Bissau's room. They stood side by side.

"After I apply the dust, we all must touch the mirror together," Bissau said.

Amber and Harriet nodded. Bissau took the dust from his pocket, then sprinkled a portion into his left hand. He lifted his palm to his mouth, then pursed his lips.

Bissau blew the dust onto the mirror. As the glass shimmered, they touched their palms against it. Amber felt warmth traveling from her palm.

"Here we go," she whispered.

CHAPTER TWENTY-ONE

Bagule stood before the home of Bahari Cole, flanked by Nieleni and Ephraim. While Nieleni's posture reflected her usual cool demeanor, Ephraim was visibly nervous. He cleared his throat before speaking.

"I shouldn't be here," he said. "It's not safe for me."

"You've come this far," Bagule said. "You might as well go all the way."

"We should go to the door," Nieleni said.

"No need," Bagule said. "What Shakira said is true. Bahari is a powerful djinn. I can feel her presence. She already knows we're here. She's trying to decide how she'll deal with us."

"I can't stay here!" Ephraim blurted. "I'm leaving!"

He was about to walk away when he froze in his tracks.

"You'll do no such thing," a woman's voice said.

Bahari Cole appeared before the door of her home. She was a stout, ebony-skinned woman with strong features. A short natural graced her head; she wore an African print dress that fell to her sandaled feet.

"What do we have here?" she said. "A djinn lover, a sorcerer and a warrior. Sounds like the beginning of a bad joke."

Bagule bowed.

"I'm honored to meet you, Bahari."

Bahari's smile faded.

"Spare me your false platitudes," she said. "Shakira told me you were coming. I suspect you were the one who entered my home three days ago."

"We did no such thing," Nieleni said.

"No one spoke to you, Servant," Bahari said.

Nieleni moved toward Bahari, but found her progress blocked by an invisible force. Bagule grinned. She was powerful.

"I can assure you it wasn't us," Bagule said. "But I know who it was."

"What difference does it make?" Bahari retorted. "Whoever it was, they came for the same thing you want."

"And what would that be?" Bagule said.

"His sword," Bahari said.

At last! Bagule struggled to remain calm. The key to his success was before him and Bahari was the only obstacle. She was powerful, very powerful, but Bagule could defeat her if it came to a fight. But he was not a man to waste power if he didn't have to.

"Tell me, how is it that you came into possession of it?"

"That's none of your business," Bahari said.

"If you would invite us in, I think we could come to an understanding about the sword."

"I don't think so," Bahari. "That sword is my insurance."

"From what?" Bagule asked.

"The Mansa," Bahari said.

Bagule's eyes went wide.

"Are you saying that the Mansa knows you have the sword?"

"Yes," Bahari answered. "It was the only thing keeping her and her horde from extending their influence to America. But apparently she sent you to do the dirty work for her."

"I owe no loyalty to the Mansa," Bagule said. "I have other intentions for the sword."

"Bagule, no," Nieleni warned.

"It's okay, Nieleni," Bagule said. "I think it's time we were all honest."

Bagule stepped forward.

"May I approach?" he asked.

"It's not like I could stop you," Bahari answered.

"True, but you would be a formidable opponent." Bagule ambled to the base of the stairs.

"I need the Mansa's help," Bagule said. "She said if I brought her the Sword of Sonni Ali, she would assist me."

"She lied," Bahari said.

"Yes, I know. However, it was never my intention to take her the sword. The prophesy says that any sorcerer possessing the sword would have control not only over humans but also djinn. With that sword I have no need for her help."

"But why would I want to give you the power to become my master?" Bahari asked.

"Because I mean you no harm," Bagule said. "I have no quarrel with the djinn, especially not those here. My interests lie thousands of miles away."

"What are you saying?" Ephraim said. The man trembled as he formed fists with his hands. "The only reason I agreed to help you was because you serve the Mansa!"

"I don't serve anyone," Bagule replied.

"The Mansa will hear of this!" Ephraim exclaimed.

"No, she won't," Bahari replied.

Bahari reached out with her hand then bunched her fingers together as if she squeezed a ball. Ephraim clutched his throat then fell to his knees.

"Shaitan take you all!" he shouted. Ephraim exploded into a white cloud.

Bahari's eyes raised.

"It seems your servant had one spell within him," she said. "He'll go straight to the Mansa."

"I'm sure he will," Bagule said, "which is why it's even more important that we join forces."

Bahari tilted her head. "What else do you want, Sorcerer?"

Bagule grinned. "You are perceptive. There is someone else that could hinder out plans."

"Who?"

"A girl," Bagule answered. "She is the great granddaughter of the Grand Djele of Marai. Her name is Amber, and she wields considerable power. Fortunately for us she does not realize how powerful she is. None of them do."

"Is she here in America?" Bahari asked.

"Yes," Bagule replied.

"Then I will prepare for her," Bahari said. "You take care of the Mansa, and I'll take care of Amber.

Bagule was extending his hand to Bahari when the door to her house burst open. A woman with shocked expression looked at Bahari.

"Sultana, there is an intruder in the secret room again!"

Bahari ran into the house.

Bagule's face twisted in consternation.

"Amber!" he hissed.

CHAPTER TWENTY-TWO

Amber, Harriet, and Bissau dropped through the void then emerged at their destination. It was not a good landing. Amber landed flat on her back, her head bumping against the floor. Bissau struck the wall, then fell to the floor. Harriet bounced off the floor, then rolled into a pedestal.

"Ow!" she exclaimed.

"Tell me about it," Amber replied.

Bissau stood as if hitting the wall was a minor inconvenience He hurried to Amber and helped her stand.

"Are you okay?" he asked.

"I've been better."

"Hey y'all, look!"

Harriet was on her feet, a big smile on her face. Beside her, on display, was Sonni Ali's sword. Amber and Bissau joined her, and they stared at the weapon in awe. Harriet took out her phone and snapped pictures as Amber reached for the protective glass.

Bissau grabbed her hand.

"Wait," he said. "We have no idea what spells may protect it. Remember what happened to me."

Amber pulled her hand back.

"How do we find out?" she asked.

"Use your Sight," Bissau answered.

"That only works on people," Amber said.

"It should work on spells as well," Bissau said. "Every spell contains the essence of its creator and the energy required to created it."

"Okay," Amber said. "I'll try."

Amber's eyes narrowed as she released her emotional vision. An intense red cloud swirled around the case.

"There's a red cloud," Amber said. "I'm glad I didn't touch it."

"Now that you can see it, you change it," Bissau said.

Amber turned to Bissau. "How do you know? I've never done anything like this before."

"You can use your ability to move things to move the spell away," Bissau said.

"How do you know?"

"That is what Master Jakada told me. He is never wrong."

"I wouldn't do that, if I were you."

Amber, Harriet and Bissau spun about. What resembled a man floated before them, his body a black silhouette, his eyes red like the spell protecting the sword case. While his upper body looked human, his lower body was swirling smoke.

"Djinn!" Bissau exclaimed. "Run!"

Harriet and Bissau hurried away in different directions. Amber stood still; her eyes locked on the djinn as it edged closer.

"You are the one," it said. "You've come for the sword. You cannot have it!"

The djinn lunged at Amber. She dodged to her left, then spun about. Reaching out with her powers, she seized the spell and threw it into the djinn's face. The djinn screamed, its hands clawing at the spell as it tightened about its head. The djinn rose through the roof of the room, still screaming.

Amber ran to the sword case and tried to lift it, but it was too heavy. She stepped away and reached out again with her powers. The case shifted, then rose slowly from the pedestal.

Amber moved it away, then gently lowered it to the floor. She went to the pedestal and wrapped her hands around the sword.

"Oh my," she whispered.

A feeling of power and confidence flowed through her arms and into her body. Never had she felt so sure of herself. She knew now why Bagule wanted the sword. It wasn't what it possessed; it was how it transformed the power within.

"You're glowing," Harriet said.

Amber looked at her arms and smiled.

"I am."

"Amber."

Amber turned. Standing on the opposite side of the room was Bagule, Nieleni and a woman she did not know. Bagule and Nieleni stared at her with malice in their eyes. The woman's expression was one of curiosity.

Bagule stepped toward her, his hands beginning to glow.

"You don't think I'm going to let you leave with that sword, do you?"

Amber gripped the hilt of the blade, then pulled it from the scabbard.

"Do you think you can stop me?" she said.

A light beam extended from Bagule's right hand then took the shape of a sword.

"We shall see," he said.

Terror struck Amber's gut. She had no idea how to fight with swords. That wasn't part of her training. Before the sorcerer could reach her, Harriet jumped in his way.

"Leave my cousin alone!" she shouted.

Bagule knocked her aside with his left hand. Harriet slammed to the ground, sliding across the floor and hitting the wall.

"Harriet!"

Amber tried to go to her, but Bagule stood between them. He attacked with the sword and Sonni Ali's sword responded, blocking his blow.

"Let the sword protect you!" Bissau shouted as he traded blows with Nieleni.

"As long as you wield it, no harm shall come to you!"

Bissau's words angered Bagule. He pressed his attack, swinging and stabbing harder. The sword matched his assault, blocking and parrying every blow. Amber slipped into her inner eye. Bissau raged red as if he was on fire as he battledNieleni, yellow lights flashing as they traded blows. Just behind Bagule, Harriet cowered against the wall, shining white in fear. Then there was the djinn, standing away and staring at her with a look of wonder on her face.

"Bahari!" Bagule shouted. "Help us!"

Amber looked at Bahari while Sonni's sword continued to protect her.

"I cannot," she said calmly. "The person who controls the sword controls me."

"Then I will have to change that!" Bagule said.

Bagule broke off his attack, then ran toward Harriet.

"No!" Amber shouted. She ran after the sorcerer.

Bissau grabbed Nieleni into a hip throw and tossed her to the ground.

"Use your gift!" Bissau shouted. "Don't . . ."

Nieleni cut him off with a kick to the jaw.

Bagule's swords disappeared as he neared Harriet.

"Amber!" Harriet screamed.

Amber reached out with her nyama. She closed her hand then lifted her arm. Harriet rose to the ceiling, avoiding Bagule's grasp by inches. Amber pulled her arm back and Harriet sailed to her; Amber lowered her arm slowly and Harriet settled behind her.

"How did you . . .?" Harriet began.

"Stay behind me," Amber said. "I got you."

Amber jerked her head toward Bissau. He laid sprawled on his back, unconscious. Nieleni stalked toward her, flexing her hand with a grim smile on her face. Bagule approached as well, his swords back in his hands. Sonni's sword lifted, ready to defend her. Amber's confidence wavered. She wasn't sure she could handle them both. Then she remembered what the djinn said.

"Bahari!" she called out. "Help me!"

The djinn appeared by her side.

"What do you wish?" she said.

"Get rid of them," Amber said.

Bahari raised her hands. Bagule and Nieleni froze.

"What are you . . ."

A grey mist appeared at Bagule's and Nieleni's feet. They tried to step away, but could not.

"What are you doing?" Amber said.

"As you asked," Bahari said. "I'm getting rid of them."

"You're not going to kill them, are you?" Harriet said.

Bahari looked at Harriet and smiled.

"I should, but I'm not. I don't think Amber would want that."

"No," Amber said. "I don't want that."

Bagule raised his hands, then pushed them down. The grey mist began to dissipate.

"You have chosen the wrong side," he said.

Bahari's arms shook. She looked to Amber.

"Help me," she said.

"How?" Amber said.

"Point the sword at Bagule," Bahari replied.

Amber raised the sword and Bagule's eyes went wide.

"Now say, begone," Bahari said.

Amber glared at Bagule.

"Begone!" she yelled.

The grey mist consumed Bagule and Nieleni like a sudden storm. Amber could see Bagule and Nieleni's mouths working but could not hear them as the smoke consumed them. When it cleared, they were gone.

"Where did you send them?" Amber asked.

"Where they wanted to go," Bahari said. "Although their arrival will not be welcomed without that."

Bahari gestured toward the sword. Amber pulled it close to her and Bahari smiled.

"Don't worry," she said. "I'm glad to be rid of it. You have no idea how frustrating it is to possess an object with such power and not be able to use it."

Amber looked at the djinn with her inner eye and saw the truth in her lavendar hue.

"Besides," Bahari continued. "Sonni Ali's sword is with the one who deserves it."

Bahari looked over her shoulder.

"You should check on your handsome friend."

Amber had forgotten about Bissau. He lay on the floor, still unconscious from Nieleni's kick. She ran to him; Harriet close behind. They both knelt beside him, staring at his swollen discolored jaw.

"That looks like it hurts," Harriet said.

"I'm sure it does, or at least it will when he comes to," Amber replied.

Bahari joined them. She placed her hand on Bissau's head then closed her eyes. A few seconds later, Bissau's eyelids fluttered. He groaned.

Bahari stepped away. Amber leaned closer to Bissau.

"Bissau?" she said.

"Amber?" he replied as he opened his eyes. He reached up and massaged his jaw.

"We defeated them?" he asked.

"Yeah, I think," Amber replied.

Amber helped Bissau sit up.

"I guess we can go home now," Harriet said. She glanced at Bahari.

"I will not try to stop you," Bahari said. "As long as you possess Sonni Ali's sword, I can't."

Bahari walked up to Amber, her eyes focusing on her namesake necklace. Her eyes widened.

"Ah, I understand now," she said.

"Understand what?" Amber replied.

"You have the necklace, and now you have the sword. There is only one more item remaining."

"Wait a minute, hold up," Amber said. "What do they have to do with each other? And what other item are you talking about?"

"Who gave you that necklace, Amber?" Bahari asked.

"My grandmother," Amber replied.

"What did she tell you about it?"

"She told me it was given to her by her father. She said it was to help her pick the next Sana of Marai. She gave it to me because it was my responsibility."

"And that is all she told you?" Bahari asked.

"Yes."

Bahari rubbed her chin. "Maybe she doesn't know."

"Doesn't know what?"

Bahari smiled. "If you grandmother did not tell you, it's not my place to do so."

Amber took out the sword.

"Tell me," she commanded.

Bahari laughed. "That won't work this time. There are some commands I don't have to obey."

Bahari looked about the room, then her eyes settled on the broken mirror. She snapped her fingers and the shattered glass rose from the floor and rattled into place.

"You can leave now," Bahari said. "I wish you all well."

Amber helped Bissau to his feet. Harriet joined them and they made their way to the mirror."

"Thank you, Bahari," Amber said. "Will we see you again?"

"I hope not," Bahari replied. "When you see your grandmother, ask her about the necklace. Ask her to tell you the whole truth."

"I told you she doesn't know," Amber said.

"Seeing you with the sword might jog her memory," Bahari said.

Bahari wiped her hand across the mirror and the glass swirled.

"Goodbye, Amber," she said.

"Goodbye, Bahari."

Amber took Bissau and Harriet's hands. She was about to step into the mirror when Bissau stopped her.

"Wait. Can we trust her?" Bissau asked.

Amber looked at Bahari with her inner eye. The djinn pulsed blue.

"Yes, we can," Amber said. "Come on. Let's go home."

Together, they stepped into the mirror.

CHAPTER TWENTY-THREE

Bagule hit the stone floor, then slid a few feet before stopping. Nieleni rolled next to him, then sprang to her feet into a fighting stance, her eyes searching the dim room where they landed. Bagule scrambled to his feet.

"Where are we?" he asked.

"I don't know," Nieleni replied.

"You are where you began," a familiar voice said.

The Mansa emerged from the darkness. As she approached the room brightened, revealing hundreds of djinn, their eyes fixed on the duo.

"So, give me the sword," the Mansa ordered.

"I don't have it," Bagule said.

The Mansa's eyes narrowed. "Then why are you here?"

Bagule hesitated before answering.

"We were . . . sent here."

"Sent here? By whom?"

"Bahari," Bagule answered.

The Mansa let out a yell that shook the room. The other djinn cowered; even Nieleni took a step back.

"She has the sword!" the Mansa said. "I suspect she has always possessed it."

"Yes," Bagule answered. "She said you knew."

"She lied," the Mansa replied. "You could not take it from her? I thought you were a powerful sorcerer. I sent one of my best servants with you."

The Mansa looked about.

"Where is he?"

"He ran away," Nieleni said. "Apparently he was not one of your best."

"Silence!"

Nieleni opened her mouth to protest, but nothing came out. Fear entered her eyes and she looked to Bagule.

"Let her go," he said.

"You are in no position to speak," the Mansa said. "You promised me Sonni Ali's sword. Instead, you return bested by Bahari without my servant."

"I was not defeated by Bahari," Bagule said. "I was beaten by the great granddaughter of Djele Jakada, grand historian of Marai. Bahari does not have Sonni Ali's sword now. She does."

"And what will she do with it?" the Mansa asked.

"Nothing," Bagule said. "Absolutely nothing. She will give it to her great grandfather, and he will hide it away to prevent anyone from using it against Marai and the Veil."

"He will let no one have it?" the Mansa asked.

"No one," Bagule replied.

The Mansa fell silent. A contemplative countenance took over her face. Then she smiled.

"Maybe my troubles are over," he said. "This girl has taken Sonni's sword. Bahari does not have it, but most of all you do not have it."

"Mansa, my only interest in the sword . . ."

"Was to obtain it so you would have control over all the djinn," the Mansa finished. "I am no fool, sorcerer. I knew your intentions. Ephraim was supposed to take the sword the moment you found it and bring it to me, alone. If not for Bahari he would have. But that is no consequence to me now. The girl has the sword; the threat to my people is gone."

"Don't be to sure," Bagule said. "This girl is a crafty one. She may come to the same conclusion I did; the only way she can truly protect Marai would be to control the djinn."

The Mansa moved closer to Bagule.

"That is not my concern at this moment," the Mansa said. "The question now is, what do I do with you?"

CHAPTER TWENTY-FOUR

Amber emerged from her bedroom mirror. Her eyes went wide and she jumped into her bed with outstretched arms.

"My bed. My beautiful, wonderful bed."

Harriet followed, with Bissau close behind. Harriet fell onto Amber's bed backward, her eyes shut tight and a big smile on her face.

"We're home!" she said.

"Keep it down!" Amber fussed.

Harriet sat up. "Why? We're already in trouble. We've been gone for two days. Your parents have probably called my parents and the police. I don't see how we're going to get out of this."

"She's right," Bissau said. "You must tell both of your parents."

There was a light knock at Amber's door.

"Amby?"

Amber cracked open the door. Mama pushed it wide, then wrapped her arms around her.

"Oh, my baby!" she said. "Where did you go?"

Mama's eyes found Harriet and she rushed and hugged her, too.

"Girl, I've been so worried about you!"

"I'm okay, Auntie," Harriet said.

"I know that now," Mama replied. She looked at Bissau and her emotions cooled.

"I'm sure your parents are worried about you, too," she said.

"They probably are," Bissau said. "I must go."

"Mama, where's Daddy?" Amber asked.

"Out looking for you," Mama said. "Both of you."

"Oh no!" Amber said.

"Oh yes," Mama replied. "We called the police yesterday. There is a missing person report out on you both. We haven't contacted Harriet's parents yet, but your daddy plans on it as soon as he returns."

"He won't have to now," Harriet said.

The door chimed. Amber felt her throat tighten. The day she dreaded was here. She would have to tell Daddy everything.

"Cindy? Are you upstairs?"

Mama took a deep breath.

"Yes, I am, Baby. I'm in Amber's room."

Amber's heart beat in time with daddy's rapid footfalls. She cringed as he grasped the doorknob, turned it, and entered the room.

"I didn't . . .Amber! Harriet!"

Daddy wrapped them both in his arms.

"You're back! We were out of our minds!"

He looked up to Mama.

"When did the police bring them back?"

"They didn't," Mama said.

Amber freed herself from Daddy's hug.

"Daddy, I need to tell you something."

"What is it Baby? Are you okay? Who is this?"

Daddy glared at Bissau. "Did this boy have something to do with you two going missing?"

Daddy came to his feet, his hands balled into fists.

"What did you do to my daughter, Boy?"

Amber and Mama jumped between them.

"Baby, I'm going to need you to sit down," Mama said. "Amber has something to tell you."

"Why is this boy in Amber's room?" Daddy asked.

"Sam, calm down," Mama said. "Amber will explain everything."

"I will not calm down!" Daddy said. "My child and my niece have been missing for two days and they show up with this boy? I can't understand why you're not upset. Did you have something to do with this, Crystal?"

"Now don't you go accusing me, Mister!" Mama said.

This was spiraling out of control.

"Mama, Daddy," Amber began. "I can explain everything."

"Maybe I should."

Amber and everyone turned to her mirror. Grandma filled the glass, a gentle smile on her face.

"What is going on?" Daddy said. "Who is this and why is she in Amber's mirror?"

"It's my Mama," Mama said.

Daddy fell onto Amber's bed. "Mama Corliss? That's impossible! She's too young to be . . . it is Mama Corliss! I don't understand."

"It's a lot to take, Sam," Grandma said. "This is all extraordinary."

"How are you talking to us through a mirror?" Daddy asked.

"It's magic!" Harriet said. "Grandma has it. So do Amber and me."

Daddy looked at Amber.

"You have magic?"

"It's not that simple," Amber said.

Daddy then turned to Mama.

"You knew about this?" he asked.

"Yes," Mama replied.

"And you're just telling me about it?"

"I found out only a few weeks ago when Amber saved me."

"Saved you?"

Daddy stood. "This is crazy. I need a drink."

"Sit down, Sam," Mama said. "Please."

"It is time you all knew everything," Grandma said. "The best way to explain it is for you all to come here."

"Where is here?" Mama asked.

"Marai," Amber answered. "Bissau?"

Bissau stepped toward the mirror, hesitating when he neared Daddy. He fell to his knees, prostrating before him.

"What are you doing?" Daddy asked.

"He's honoring you," Amber said.

"Forgive me, Baba," Bissau said. "I can understand your anger. I can assure you that I have brought no harm to your daughter. My duty is and will always be to protect her."

"Uh . . . what is he talking about?" Daddy asked.

Bissau stood, then went to Harriet.

"Take my hand," he said.

Harriet giggled. "Okay."

Harriet took Bissau's hand.

"Are you ready?" Bissau asked.

Harriet nodded. Together then jumped into the mirror and disappeared. Daddy's mouth fell open.

"They just . . ."

Amber took Daddy and Mama's hands.

"What are you doing, Amby?" Mama asked.

"Trust me," Amber said.

She led them to the mirror. Amber wasn't sure they would take the leap, so she wrapped her *ka* around them, then lifted them off their feet.

"Here we go," she whispered.

Amber took her parents through the mirror.

* * *

Sam and Cindy stood in the study of Baba Jakada. The grand djele sat on his stool, a welcoming smile on his face. Corliss and Bissau stood on either side of him, Bissau still holding Harriet's hand. Cindy's and Sam's stunned expressions were reflected in the others.

"Where are we?" Mama said.

"You are in Marai," Corliss said.

Bissau's head jerked about.

"Where is Amber? Bissau said.

CHAPTER TWENTY-FIVE

Something was wrong. Amber fell through the mysterious realm between mirrors far long than she ever had. Strange forces played a game of tug of war with her, pulling her in every direction. Everything hurt and she cried out a few times in response. After a few more moments, the pulling subsided. The pressure of the journey finally relented and her feet touched the ground. Her knees gave way and she collapsed on the cold floor beneath her.

"Is this her?" a distant strange voice said.

"Yes," another voice responded. She recognized it, but could not determine who in her weakened state.

"Take them both away," the first voice commanded. "I will deal with them when I am ready."

A pair of hands gripped her arms, then jerked her from the floor. Whoever held her dragged her for a long time, then placed her on a cushioned surface. She heard a door slam, then a loud click. Wherever she was, she had been locked inside.

"Who are you?" she managed to say. "Where am I?"

"There is no use in all that," someone said. "We are prisoners. It is your fault, stupid girl."

Another voice Amber recognized. She sat up and shook her head. Her vision slowly returned. Two people sat opposite her, their features sharper with every second. When her sight finally returned, she gasped.

"Bagule! Nieleni!"

A smile formed on Bagule's face. Nieleni glared at her.

"Amber Robinson," Bagule said. "Here we are again."

Amber tried to stand, but was jerked back to her cushion. She looked at her ankles; shackles encircled them.

"What did you do to me?"

"I didn't do anything," Bagule said. "This is all your fault. If you didn't stop me from acquiring Sonni Ali's sword, we wouldn't be prisoners of the Djinn Mansa."

Amber was confused. "Prisoners of who?"

"It doesn't matter," Bagule said. "We are here now, and we will probably be here until we die."

Bagule's last words struck her cold.

"Until we die?"

"Yes," Bagule said."

Amber tugged at her bonds. It was then she noticed her necklace was gone.

"Who took my necklace?"

"That is the least of your worries," Bagule replied. "The Mansa has the sword of Sonni Ali, thanks to you. There is nothing that can stop her now."

"Stop her from what?" Amber asked.

"Destroying Marai."

Amber leaned back against the stone wall behind her. She closed her eyes and concentrated. The bonds around her ankles and wrists vibrated as she strained to break them. A wave of fatigue hit her and she relented.

"Impressive," Bagule said. "Especially without your precious necklace."

"I don't see you doing anything," Amber said.

"I'm saving my strength," Bagule replied. "Tell me, if you were to break your bonds, what would you do next?"

Amber's shoulders slumped.

"I don't know," she admitted.

Bagule grinned. "Exactly. You have power, but power is useless if it's not used judiciously. It's a shame we're rivals. There is so much I could teach you."

"I don't need your help," Amber said. "I have my grand-mother and great-grandfather."

"Yes, you do, yet here you are sitting in the Djinn Mansa's dungeon."

"With you," Amber said.

Bagule looked thoughtful. "You have a point. So, we must determine why the Mansa his holding us, and if there will be an opportunity for escape."

"We?" Amber said. "Why should I work with you? You hate me and my family. You're trying to destroy us!"

Bagule sighed. "Hate is a strong word. Now I will admit I don't have any pleasant feelings about your great-grandfather. The man is a liar and a tyrant."

"No, he isn't!" Amber shouted.

"Are you sure? You barely know him. I, however, have toler-ated his pompous personality for centuries."

A kernel of doubt formed in Amber's mind. Everything she knew about Baba was through her grandmother. She loved him, yet she escaped Marai to get away from him and her responsi-bility. Bissau admired him, but his feelings seemed to come more from duty than emotion. Then she thought back to the tribunal. There were many Maraibu that agreed with Bagule to lift the Veil.

"She's beginning to think on her own," Bagule said to Nieleni.

"Yes," Nieleni replied.

"Be quiet," Amber said.

"I bear no ill will toward you or your grandmother," Bagule said. "We just happen to be on opposite sides."

"You tried to kill me," Amber said.

"It was a last resort, and if you must know, I felt bad about that," Bagule said.

"Stop talking. I'm not listening anymore." Amber wanted to curl up and sleep, but her shackles wouldn't allow it.

"No matter how you feel about me, the only way we'll have a chance to get out of this place is to work together," Bagule said. "The sooner you realize it, the sooner we can devise a plan."

The lock on their door rattled then it swung open. Two djinn draped in chainmail and headwraps entered. Amber gasped when she noticed they had no legs, just a spiraling smoke that rose to their torsos. They cut glances at Bagule and Nieleni, then approached Amber. One of the guards pointed its spear at Amber and her shackles fell free.

"Come with us," she said.

Amber stood and the djinns flanked her. Together, they walked out of the dungeon.

"We will talk again when you return," Bagule called out. "If you return."

One of the guards turned to Bagule.

"Be quiet," he said.

A gag appeared in Bagule's mouth. The djinns laughed. One of the djinn grasped Amber's arm, then led her into the corridor. The dungeon door slammed and Amber jumped. For some reason, she felt safer inside it than she did in the hall with the djinn. Bagule was an enemy, but at least he was familiar.

Amber walked down the passageway with the djinn, taking in what she had missed on her first trip to the dungeon. The walls of the corridor were incredibly high, as if beings much larger than her traversed it. They were covered with strange art unlike any Amber had ever seen, some images familiar, others completely alien. They made a sharp right turn, entering a smaller hallway with an alabaster plain wall. At the end of the passage was a simple door made of what looked like gold. The djinn grasped the gilded handles, then opened the door. One of them gestured with its head.

"Inside," it ordered.

"No," Amber replied. "I don't know what's in there."

The djinn's smile was not reassuring. "You are safe for now. Please enter."

"No," Amber said.

The djinn's smile faded. It nodded its head; Amber blacked out for a second. When her sight returned, she was sitting on the floor on other side of the portal. The door was closed.

"Come forward," a booming voice commanded.

Amber turned her attention to the figure sitting in a massive throne on the opposite side of the room. The Djinn Mansa sat alone, flanked by two statues that resembled those from ancient Kemet. She wore a billowing gold and purple dress that shimmered like metal. A towering headwrap the same colors crowned her head. Dozens of beaded necklaces hung from her neck and golden bracelets encircled her wrists and ankles. Amber took a deep breath then ambled to the Mansa. As she neared, she saw the two familiar objects; Sonni Ali's sword and her amber necklace.

Amber halted a few feet away from the Mansa. The Mansa's eyes narrowed as she studied Amber, then to Amber's surprise, a smile came to her face.

"You are too young to have such a powerful talisman in your possession," she said.

"It depends on who you ask," Amber replied.

The Mansa laughed, a loud boisterous sound that echoed throughout the cavernous room.

"I like you," the Mansa said. "Unlike the other two. They sought to outwit me. They failed."

It was Amber's turn to laugh. She covered her mouth in a poor attempt to hide her mirth.

The Mansa's expression turned serious.

"I know why the sorcerer wants Sonni Ali's sword. Why do you wish to possess it?"

"I don't," Amber replied. "To be honest, I wish I never heard of it. I was after it to keep Bagule from getting it and destroying the Veil that protects Marai."

"Protect Marai?" The Mansa rubbed her chin. "That's an interesting way to describe it."

"What do you mean?" Amber asked.

"There are many things you do not know of this world, or our world," the Mansa replied. "You've been told half-truths and, in some cases, complete falsehoods. Take this necklace, for instance."

The Mansa held up her necklace.

"You have no clue how powerful this charm is. If you did, I would be bowing at your feet."

"I don't want that," Amber said. "I don't want any of this. I just want to help my great grandfather, then go home."

The Mansa leaned back into her throne.

"I'm not sure if you really mean that, or if you're just as crafty as Bagule. You humans are a sneaky lot."

The Mansa fell silent, rolling Amber's necklace between her fingers.

"I must think on this," she finally said.

The djinn who escorted her to the Mansa appeared beside her.

"Take her back to the dungeon," the Mansa said.

Amber's shoulders slumped, tears forming in her eyes.

"Please," she said. "I just want to go home."

"Take her away," the Mansa repeated.

The djinn escorted her through the gilded door and into the hallway.

"That wasn't so bad," one of the djinn said.

Amber jerked her head to the djinn.

"What are you talking about? I'm in a prison!"

"Yes, you are," the other djinn replied. "However, the Mansa is still deciding if you will remain so."

"I hope she makes up her mind soon," Amber said.

"We'll see," the djinn said.

They reached Amber's cell. The door opened and Amber stepped inside. As she entered, the gag disappeared from Bagule's mouth.

"I see you are still with us," he said.

Amber said nothing. She went to sit on her bench. To her relief, the shackles did not reappear on her ankles and wrists.

"It seems the Mansa no longer sees you as a threat, which is the perfect opportunity to escape."

"She's considering releasing me," Amber said.

"Oh, she used that one on you," Bagule said. "Amber, the Djinn Mansa is virtually immortal. She may decide to release you tomorrow or one hundred years from now. You have a choice; wait for a reprieve that may never come, or use your limited freedom to plan an escape with us."

Amber's mind swirled in confusion. She no more wanted to team up with Bagule and Nieleni than she wanted a hole in her head. But she had no idea what the Mansa would decide. Amber raised her hands, then sat down hard.

"What's your plan?" she asked.

CHAPTER TWENTY-SIX

Britani locked her bike on the sky-blue bike rack outside the entrance of Bottom Creek Park. Today would be a good day, because it would be her first time seeing Bissau since the end of the school year. Cars and vans packed the parking lot for the first games of summer league soccer. Parents, family, and friends of the players ambled to the entrance carrying coolers, folding chairs, and backpacks, sharing a jovial mood despite the hot morning. It would get hotter later that day, but Britani didn't mind. She loved the heat.

As she inched her way to the entrance, her mood dampened a bit. The truth was Bissau wasn't playing summer league; Amber was. And wherever you found Amber, you found Bissau. Although they insisted they weren't interested in each other. Britani knew better. She knew denial when she saw it. It wasn't on Bissau's part. She knew he liked Amber more than he let on because he talked about her too much when they were together. It was Amber who wouldn't admit her feelings. For some reason she didn't want to like Bissau, and that was fine with Britani. The longer she put him off, the more time Britani had to get his attention.

Bottom Creek Park consisted of six soccer fields. Each would have a game in progress, from small children to summer league players like Amber. Britani paid the entry fee, then worked her way to the opposite side of the park where the summer league games would take place. The summer league was for the serious soccer players, players like Amber who had aspirations of playing in college or maybe even pro. Britani didn't think that far ahead.

Unlike her friends, Britani wasn't consumed with the game. She'd taken up the game recently and discovered she had a knack for it. She was a better than average player, but would never be a superstar like Amber. But she didn't really want to be.

As soon as she reached the summer league fields, she began her search for Bissau. She scanned the crowd as she politely pushed her way through it. She didn't know which team Amber playing for but if she could find out and where they would play first, she would find Bissau. She was passing by a girls team when she heard a familiar name; Jasmine. Britani searched the girls and spotted the one they were speaking to. Britani recognized Amber's best friend from the pictures on her phone. Britani made her way to the girl.

"Hey, Jasmine!" she said. "What's up, girl?"

Jasmine looked at Britani with a frown.

"Do I know you?" she said.

"No. My name is Britani. We have a mutual friend; Amber Robinson."

Jasmine's eyes brightened. "Ah, okay. She's mentioned you a few times. You're from Cuba, right?"

"Yes," Britani said. "Amber and I used to play together at Clifton Academy before she quit the team."

"Yeah, that was a tough situation," Jasmine said. "Hey, have you talked to Amber lately? I've been trying to reach her. She missed all our practices this week."

It was Britani's turn to be surprised.

"Really? I was sure she would be here."

"She's not, and Coach ain't happy," Jasmine said.

Britani suddenly lost all interest in the game.

"Well, if I see her, I'll tell her everybody is looking for her. Nice to meet you, Jasmine. Maybe you, me, and Amber can hang out sometime."

"Yeah, sure," Jasmine said. "Hey, I got to go. Game is starting soon."

Britani waved, then hurried away, her forced smile becoming a frown. Bissau would not be at the games. She wasted her time coming. But where was Amber?

Britani exited the park, got her bike, and pedaled away. She headed for another destination, a place where she shouldn't go but was going to anyway. Desperate times called for desperate measures. A half an hour later she rode up to Bissau's apartment complex. She had no idea how he would feel seeing her at his home, but she knew how he would react. Bissau was always the gentleman, so if he was angry, he wouldn't show it. That would give her time to calm him down with her charm. At least she hoped that would be how it went.

She skirted around the gate and the empty guardhouse, then hurried to his apartment. Britani knocked on the door, then tapped her foot as she waited for an answer. There was none. She knocked again; a bit harder. Still, no answer.

Something's not right, Britani thought. There was one more stop to make; Amber's home.

Britani climbed on her bike, then pedaled to Amber's house. Fortunately for her, Bissau and Amber didn't live too far from each other. She reached Amber's neighborhood and worked her way through the joggers and dog walkers getting their steps in before the summer's heat made it unbearable.

Britani finally reached Amber's home. She parked her bike then walked up to the front door and rang the doorbell. There was no answer. Britani peeked into the windows to see if she could see anyone inside.

"Hi there!"

Britani turned toward the voice. A tall brown man wearing an Atlanta Falcons t-shirt and cargo shorts stood at the edge of his immaculate yard, his arms folded across his chest and a suspicious look on his face.

"Hi!" Britani replied. She ambled to her bike, then walked it down the driveway.

"I'm Britani, a friend of Amber's," she said. "I was just visiting."

"The Robinson's are out of town, I believe," the man said. "Although they didn't let anyone know they were leaving."

"Really?" Britani said.

"Yes," the man replied. "We look out for each other, which is why I'm out here. I saw you peeking into their window."

"I'm sorry," Britani said. "It's a bad habit. Sometimes people are home and don't hear the doorbell."

"Um hm," the man said. "Well, I'll tell them you dropped by when I see them."

"Thanks!"

Britani rode away, the man in the yard watching her until she was out of sight. She kept riding until she reached her own home, a quaint house across the street from Grant Park. Britani rusheds into the house, running up the stairs to her bedroom. Something was wrong. Not only were Amber and Bissau missing, but so was Amber's family. Britani went to her closet, taking out an outfit she hadn't worn in a long time. She knew her charade would end one day, but this was sooner than expected. As she changed her clothes, her appearance changed as well. Britani Haddish disappeared, replaced by Aisha.

"If both of you are missing, I know exactly where you are," Aisha said. "It's time to return to Marai."

CHAPTER TWENTY-SEVEN

Alake stroked Crystal's hair as her daughter cried into her lap. She'd been inconsolable since the day Amber disappeared within the mirror, as was everyone else. Sam paced, still trying to comprehend what was happening around him. Jakada spent every waking moment with the mirrors, trying to locate his great granddaughter. Harriet slept, waking only to eat and relieve herself.

But it was Bissau who worried her the most. He took full responsibility for Amber's disappearance. Every day, he entered the mirrors, physically searching for her. Even after Jakada's command for him to stop, he continued. It was the first time she ever saw him defy her father. Alake couldn't let things continue the way they were going. She had to do something.

"Get up, Peaches," she said. "Come with me."

"What?" Crystal asked.

"Don't question me," Alake said.

Crystal lifted her head from Alake's lap, then rubbed her eyes. Alake stood then pulled Crystal up to her feet. She held her hand and led her out of the room to Sam's room. Sam stopped pacing, looking at them with desperation in his eyes.

"Did you find her?" he asked.

"No," Alake replied. "But I need you to come with me."

"Okay," Sam said.

The three of them walked down the hallway to the room where Harriet slept. Alake went to her bedside, then gently shook her until she woke. Harriet rubbed her eyes, then shared a sweet smile.

"What's up, Grandma?" she asked.

"Come with me, Baby," Alake said.

"I'm sleepy," Harriet replied.

"I know, Baby," this won't take long.

Harriet stretched then yawned. "Okay."

Harriet followed her into the hallway and joined the others. Alake didn't stop by Bissau's bedroom; she knew he wouldn't be there. Instead, she went to the small parlor where Jakada kept one of his mirrors. Bissau sat slumped before the mirror, his eyes transfixed on its shimmering surface.

"Bissau," she said. "I need you to come with me."

"I can't," Bissau replied without moving. "I must find Amber."

"That's what we're going to do," Alake said. "But I need you with us to do so."

Bissau turned his head. Heavy bags hung under his blood-shot eyes as he forced a grin to his face.

"How do you expect to do that?" Bissau asked. "I've looked everywhere."

"Just come with us," Alake said.

Bissau stood then trudged behind her into the hall. Alake led everyone into Jakada's main chamber. Her father stood before his mirror, gesturing with his hands as he moved the shifting forces before him.

"Baba," she said.

Jakada turned to face her.

"What is it, Alake?"

"I need your attention for a moment," she said.

Jakada looked over her shoulder.

"I see you have assembled everyone."

"Yes."

Jakada waved his hand across the mirror and the swirling ended.

"Everyone, sit please," he said.

They all sat except for Alake. She took a moment to share a comforting smile with them before speaking.

"We are all upset, and for good reason," she said. "Amber has been missing for days, and there is no sign of her so far."

Crystal began crying again. Sam wrapped his arm around her shoulder then pulled her close.

"Each of us have handled the loss differently and separately," Alake said. "But it is time we came together to figure out what happened and where she may be."

"My, my; isn't this a somber group."

Alake's attention went to the room entrance. Leaning against the wall with a smirk on her face was Aisha. Bissau jumped to his feet and marched toward her."

"You!" he called out. "What are you doing here? How did you get inside?"

"I'm a shapeshifter," Aisha replied. "How do you think I got in? As for why I'm here, it was the logical place to come when I discovered Amber and Bissau were missing. By the way, where is Amber?"

Alake blocked Bissau with her arm before he reached Aisha.

"How did you know they were missing?" Alake asked.

"Well, when Amber didn't show up for her game and Bissau was missing from his apartment, I realized something was amiss."

Bissau's eyes widened. "How do you know what was happening in Atlanta?"

Aisha's smile grew wider as her face transformed. Moments later everyone gazed at the face of Britani.

Alake had to grab Bissau to keep him from attacking Aisha.

"That's what I like about you, Bissau," she said. "So full of fire."

Crystal moved closer to Aisha, then frowned.

"I knew something wasn't right about that girl," she said.

"If there's someone not right, it's your daughter," Aisha replied. "Look at how much trouble she's caused. Where is she, by the way?"

"We don't know," Harriet said.

"Really?" Aisha said. "Now this is interesting. Tell me more."

"Don't tell her anything," Bissau said. "She serves Bagule."

"I serve the highest bidder. You should know that by now," Aisha said. "And you should tell me everything. I may be able to find her."

Alake looked at her father and he shrugged.

"Aisha can do nothing to make our situation worse. Tell her."

"No!" Bissau shouted.

Jakada approached Bissau, grasped his shoulders then turned him to face him.

"Bissau, I have tolerated your disrespect because I know you are grieving. That ends today. I am your mentor. You will do as I say."

Bissau dropped his head. "I apologize, Uncle. I have let my emotions overrule my manners. It will not happen again."

Bissau cut his eyes at Aisha, then sat.

Alake told Aisha everything that had occurred up the moment Amber disappeared. The more she explained, the more Aisha's smile grew. By the time she finished, Aisha was laughing.

"I don't see what's so funny," Crystal said. "My only child is missing and you're laughing?"

"I apologize, Mrs. Robinson," Aisha said. "I'm laughing because I know exactly where Amber is."

All eyes fell on Aisha.

"Where is she?" Crystal asked. "Where's my baby/"

"The Djinn Mansa has her," Aisha replied. "And I know where she resides."

"How do you know she has her?" Bissau asked. "And how do you know where to find her?"

"There is only one being who would want Sonni Ali's sword more than Bagule, and that would be the Mansa," Aisha answered. "Once Amber took possession of the sword, the Djinn Mansa knew her location. As for why I know where she is; how do you think I'm able to do what I do?"

Bagule stepped back.

"You're a djinn!"

"Not exactly," Aisha said. "I'm half-djinn. My mother is djinn and my father human. I spent my childhood in the djinn kingdom but left as soon as I became an adult."

"Why did you leave?" Alake asked.

Aisha's face became solemn.

"Let's just say it's easier to be half djinn among humans."

"So, when can we go and bring Amber back?" Crystal asked.

Aisha's ever-present smirk returned.

"I see you don't know me very well, Mrs. Robinson."

"How much will it cost us?" Jakada asked.

"Make me an offer," Aisha replied. "And don't scrimp. Whatever the amount, you need to make sure Bagule can't match it."

"How do we know you won't ask the Djinn Mansa the same?" Bissau said.

"I have my reasons," Aisha said. "You'll just have to trust me."

"Trust you?" Bissau sucked his teeth.

"One more request," Aisha said.

"What is that?" Alake asked.

"A kiss on the cheek from Bissau."

Everyone turned to Bissau. He came to his feet and stomped up to Aisha. As he leaned in to kiss her cheek, she transformed her face to Britani then jerked her head around. Bissau kissed her lips. His eyes flew open when he realized what she had done. Aisha laughed as Bissau stumbled away.

"And now that story is complete," Aisha said. "Britani finally gets what she longed for."

"Three baskets of gold," Jakada said. "It is all that I have."

"That will suffice," Aisha said. "And since I know you are a man of your word, I will not ask for payment until I return with Amber. If I return."

"If?" Crystal asked.

"I'm not well-liked in the Djinn Mansadom," Aisha said. "This will be an interesting adventure."

Aisha stepped back into the hallway and disappeared before anyone could protest.

"This is it?' Sam asked. "This is all we can do?"

"Yes," Alake replied. "That, and pray."

CHAPTER TWENTY-EIGHT

Bagule gazed at the mystical chains holding him to the hard bench, then grinned. He closed his eyes, searching inside himself and found what he sought. It was time. Nieleni noticed his expression and grinned.

"Are you ready?" she asked.

Bagule opened his eyes. "Yes. Time to claim the sword and be rid of this place."

"What about Amber?" Nieleni asked.

"A minor obstacle," Bagule replied. "Although she had Maraibu blood, she is unskilled and undisciplined. I will deal with her once and for all."

"But the Mansa will help her," Nieleni said.

"That is why we must obtain the sword first. When I possess it, the Mansa and all of her followers will be useless. They will bow to their new master, and we will march on Marai."

"We'll have to find it first," Nieleni said.

"I know exactly where it is," Bagule replied.

Bagule's hands balled into fists then glowed. The shackles on his wrists popped free, as did those around his ankles. He walked to Nieleni, touching her shackles with his index finger. Her shackles opened, then fell to the floor. Nieleni stood, rubbing her wrists.

"One more thing," Bagule said.

He placed his finger on Nieleni's forehead. The woman shook, then staggered. She threw out her hands, catching herself on the wall.

"What did you do to me?" she said.

"Shared a bit of my power," Bagule replied.

Nieleni smirked as she flexed her fingers. Bagule nodded at the wall; Nieleni made fists, then punched the stone, knocking out large chunks. She studied her unbruised hands then smiled.

"Excellent!" she said.

"It's time we claimed a sword," Bagule said.

They marched toward the cell door. Nieleni shuffled forward, then kicked the door off its hinges. Angry guards blocked the entrance, their spears lowered. Nieleni stepped aside just as a ball of light shot from Bagule's hands. The djinn guards burst into whisps of smoke.

Bagule looked left and right as his senses sought out which direction they should proceed. He finally looked to his right.

"This way," he said.

Bagule and Nieleni strode down the halls of the Djinn palace. The palace servants scattered as they approached. More guards challenged them to no avail as they neared the throne room. Bagule dispersed them with his power; those that managed to slip by were dealt with by Nieleni. Soon the palace rang with the calls and cries of its inhabitants. Bagule ran.

"We must hurry!" he said.

They reached the hall leading to the throne room and were met by a large contingent of palace guards. Bagule stopped then nodded at Nieleni.

"Ayyyeeee!" Nieleni shouted, running at the guards.

The guards echoed her yell and advanced, their shields and spears lowered. Just before they clashed Nieleni leaped over their shield wall, landing in their midst. In seconds, she stripped the weapons from two guards and become a whirlwind of death among them. Bagule stood ready to aid her, but soon realized that would not be necessary. Whatever frustrations his companion had held in during their quest of for Sonni Ali's sword were being unleashed on the Mansa's guards. The last guard standing tried her best, but she was no match for Nieleni. For some reason Nieleni spared her, striking her on the head with the blunt end of her spear and knocking the guard unconscious.

Nieleni stepped through the scattered bodies, then attempted to open the chamber door. Even with her enhanced strength, the door did not budge.

"Stand aside," Bagule said.

Nieleni backed away from the entrance. Bagule raised his arms over his head, his palms facing each other. He closed his eyes and concentrated. A white sphere of energy formed between his hands until it filled the space. Bagule pulled his arms back, then threw the sphere at the door. The orb hit the door then exploded, sending shards and debris flying everywhere. The force knocked both Bagule and Nieleni off their feet, Nieleni hitting the nearby wall. Bagule struck the floor, then slid. He came to his feet. Nieleni pulled herself to her feet against the wall. She glared at Bagule.

"The next time you plan to do something like that, give me a warning."

Bagule grinned as he took her arm. Together they entered the Mansa's chamber, braced for whatever obstacles would come their way. Bagule was disappointed by its appearance, expecting the space to be much more opulent than it appeared. Those thoughts became insignificant as he realized two things; the chamber was empty, and he knew the location of the sword.

Bagule bypassed the Mansa's throne, striding directly to what seemed to be a bare wall. He pressed his palm against it and a door formed. With a sudden push, the door opened to the Mansa's private chambers. It was there the Mansa kept her treasures; the room was filled with rugs, jewels, precious metals and art from the corners of the world. Laying on the Mansa's bed was the sword. The Mansa hadn't bothered to hide it, so confident was she in her power. Bagule sauntered to the weapon, its power drawing him like a moth to light. He knelt as he wrapped his hands around the scabbard and the sword hilt. With a jerk he unsheathed the sword and was hit with a rush of power that blinded it him for a moment. When his eyes cleared, he laughed.

"At last," he said.

Nieleni stood beside him. She ran her fingers along the blade and smiled.

"Our ascension begins," she said.

"Yes, it does," Bagule replied. "It's time we found the Mansa and Amber. They must be dealt with."

"First, them," Nieleni said.

"Then, Marai," Bagule finished.

CHAPTER TWENTY-NINE

Amber woke to the click of her door lock. She rubbed her eyes as she sat up in the voluptuous bed that had been her resting place for the last week. Her eyes cleared to revealing the massive room filled with Asian designed dressers and drawers. Carpets and paintings from around the world and throughout time covered the walls, each complementing each other and creating a sight that rivaled the best museums in the world. Yet it was still a prison.

Jukunda, her djinn companion, drifted to her holding a tray full of fruit. He smiled at her pleasantly as always.

"Good morning, Amber," he said. "I hope this day finds you in good spirits."

"I'm a prisoner, Jukunda," Amber replied. "There's nothing good about that."

Jukunda set the tray over Amber's lap. The sight of the food took the edge off of Amber's mood. She picked up her fork and knife, then dove in.

"You were a prisoner," Jukunda said. "Now you are an involuntary guest. It is an improvement."

"Hooray," Amber said with her mouth full.

"You must be patient," Jukunda said. "You are slowly gaining the Mansa's trust. Once she feels you are an ally, she will set you free."

"In the meantime, my family is worried sick about me," Amber said. "They probably think I'm dead."

Jukunda's hand flew to his mouth.

"Oh my! I never considered that."

"I'm sure you didn't," Amber replied. "Neither did your Mansa. Maybe she doesn't care."

"You should ask her," Jukunda said.

Amber finished off the last of her breakfast.

"Ask her what?"

"If you could contact your family and let them know you in good health."

"I'll ask her to let me go," she said. "Like I do every day."

Jukunda smiled. "Today might be that day."

"Or it might not," Amber said.

The door opened again as Jukunda picked up her tray. Her escort to the Mansa entered.

"The Mansa has some kind of security system," Amber commented.

"The Mansa knows all that occurs in her realm," Jukunda replied. "You should be mindful of this."

Amber understood the meaning of Jukunda's words.

"Thank you," Amber said.

The guards approached.

"Amber, the Mansa requests your presence."

"I know, I know," Amber replied. "Will all of you please leave so I can get dressed?"

Jukunda and the guards left the room. Amber went into the washroom attached to her bedroom, washing up and donning the clothes the Mansa provided for her. She looked in the mirror and laughed.

"I look like a movie princess," she said.

She ambled to the door and knocked; the guards opened it, then she followed them to the Mansa's audience chamber. The Mansa greeted her with a warm smile.

"Amber! How are you today?"

"Still in prison," Amber replied.

The Mansa laughed.

"I like your sense of humor," she said.

"That wasn't a joke," Amber replied.

The Mansa stood, then strode to her.

"Come with me," she said. "I have something to show you."

Amber followed the Mansa into the corridor. She realized after the second day of her tours that the palace was much larger than it appeared on the outside. Whether it was reality or magic, she didn't know.

"Jukunda told me you know everything that happens inside the palace," Amber said.

"Jukunda exaggerates," the Mansa replied.

"So, you didn't listen when I was imprisoned with Bagule and Nieleni?"

"Of course, I did," the Mansa answered. "That's why I separated you."

"I would think you would have put me in worse conditions," Amber said.

"You are not the problem," the Mansa said. "Bagule is. I don't think you mean us harm."

The Mansa reached into her robe pocket and pulled out Amber's necklace.

"A show of good faith," she said. "Allow me."

Amber stopped walking so the Mansa could fasten the necklace around her neck. Feeling its warmth against her skin lifted her confidence.

"Thank you," she said.

"It was never mine to keep," the Mansa replied. "This was passed down to you from your ancestors."

Their walk ended before a pair of large gilded doors. The Mansa nodded and the doors opened. The room was an enormous library with shelves that rose to its domed ceiling.

"This is the history of the djinn," the Mansa said. "I've read every book."

"Impossible!" Amber said. "There's probably a million books here!"

"One million, three hundred seventy-five thousand, four hundred and eight, to be exact," the Mansa said.

Amber looked skeptical. "And you've read every last one."

"Yes," the Mansa replied.

"All of them," Amber said.

"Yes," the Mansa repeated.

"From beginning to end?" Amber said.

The Mansa smirked. "I may have skimmed through a few."

"I thought so," Amber replied.

"That's why I like you, Amber," the Mansa said. "No one in my realm would question my word."

"And that's the reason to keep me around? To question you?"

The Mansa sighed. "I am being selfish. I know you're not a threat to us. I sensed it the day you came to us."

"I didn't come here on my own," Amber said. "I had help."

"See, that's what makes you special," the Mansa said. "There was once someone else like you, but she's been gone a long time now."

"Who was that?" Amber asked.

"Me."

Amber and the Mansa turned toward the voice. Amber's eyes went wide as she recognized the woman sauntering to them.

"Aisha," she said.

"Amber," Aisha replied. "Always showing up where you don't belong."

Aisha grinned at the Mansa."

"Hello, Aunt," she said. "It's been a long time."

"Centuries," the Mansa replied. "I am happy to see you."

"Are you?" Aisha's smile faded. "Don't get comfortable. I'm here for her, nothing more."

Amber's eyes narrowed.

"For me? Who's paying you?"

"Your great grandfather," Aisha said. "And your boyfriend Bissau gave me a kiss to seal the deal. Or should I say he kissed Britani."

Aisha flashed Britani's face and Amber scowled.

"You ain't got no shame," she said.

"None at all," Aisha replied.

"What makes you think I'll free her?" the Mansa asked.

"Because you don't need to keep her now that I've returned," Aisha said. "I have so much to share with you."

"I've always been fond of your stories," the Mansa said. "You remind me so much of your mother when you tell them."

Aisha's face darkened. "Don't speak of her that way. You have no right to."

"I have the right to speak of my sister. How long are you going to blame me?" the Mansa said.

Amber heard the pain in her voice. She gazed at the Mansa with her second sight and saw her regret as deep blue. The Mansa glanced and Amber and suddenly Amber was embarrassed.

"She can't leave unless you agree to stay," the Mansa said.

"That's not the agreement I have," Aisha said. "We both leave together."

"What if I pay you to stay?" the queen asked.

"You are desperate," Aisha replied. "There's not enough wealth to keep me here."

"Aisha, listen to . . ."

Nyima swayed, them stumbled. She grabbed her forehead, then her eyes widened.

"No!" she exclaimed. "How could they?"

"What's happening?" Amber asked.

"Bagule," the Mansa replied. "He has Sonni Ali's sword. He's coming here."

Amber's stomach churned. "How did he escape?"

"I don't know," Nyima replied. "Worse, I didn't sense it."

"This is not my fight," Aisha said. "Good luck to you."

"Aisha, wait!" the Mansa called out. "You must help defend your home. You are only half djinn. The sword has no effect on you."

Aisha glowered. "Only half djinn? This place means nothing to me."

Aisha faded into nothingness. Amber and Nyima stared at where she had been.

The queen placed her hand on Amber's shoulders.

"You must be ready."

"Me? What can I do?"

"Bagule has the sword," the Mansa explained. "When he arrives, I'll be at his command. My will is strong enough that he will not be able to force me to attack you, but I won't be able to help you."

Amber's breathing became short.

"But how will I be able to stop him?"

"You have your necklace," Nyima replied. "It has the power."

An explosion rocked the chamber. Amber stumbled, bumping into the Mansa. When Amber looked at the ruler, she stood still, her eyes glazed. Amber was alone.

"It seems the tables have turned."

Bagule and Nieleni emerged from the smoke. Bagule held Sonni Ali's sword, a triumphant smile on his face. Nieleni ambled beside him, flexing her fingers. Amber's second sight displayed them both red with anger as her necklace warmed. She felt the energy flow throughout her body, yet still she was unsure.

"Bissau, I wish you were here," she whispered.

Bagule's eyes shifted to the Mansa.

"Apprehend her," he ordered.

Nyima's arms lifted, then snapped back to her side. The Mansa was fighting his commands, but Amber did not know how long that would last. She had no choice. She couldn't run; she had to fight.

"Nieleni!" Bagule shouted.

Nieleni let out an ear-piercing scream, then charged at Amber. As she neared, all of Amber's anxiety and apprehension faded away. Her mind shifted as it did at the beginning of a soccer game. Everything Bissau and Grandma taught her ran through her head in a flash. She was as ready as she'd ever be.

Nieleni's attack was powerful and full of anger. Amber deftly blocked and avoided her punches and kicks, her necklace flashing with each contact. Amber noticed Nieleni's color faded with each blow. After a few moments, Nieleni noticed it, too. She stepped back, confusion on her face.

"Bagule, something's not . . ."

Amber reached out with her nyama, lifted Nieleni off her feet, then threw her across the room. She sailed over Bagule, struck the floor, then slid back to the entrance. Bagule followed Nieleni with his eyes, turning away from Amber. When he turned his head back, his face was twisted with rage.

"Insolent girl!" he growled.

He swung the sword and an arc of light sped toward Amber. Amber crossed her arms, forming a shield before her. The light struck the shield and Amber stumbled backward. The contact felt like a jolt of static electricity. Bagule continued his attack, swinging the sword and moving closer to Amber with each stroke. Amber avoided some of the strikes and absorbed others, the pain increasing with each contact. She couldn't take much more.

An idea popped in her head. She glanced toward the fallen guards, then reached out for one of their shields with her nyama. The shield lifted from the floor, then streaked toward Bagule. It was about to collide with his head when he sidestepped, avoiding the blow.

"Dang it!" Amber exclaimed. She caught the shield, then slid it onto her left arm. At least it would help deflect the bolts.

Bagule continued to advance until he was close enough to Amber to strike her with the sword. As he raised his arm, a flash of heat and light exploded from Amber's necklace, blinding her.

When her sight returned, Bagule loomed over her, the sword raised over her head. Amber braced herself for the blow, but Bagule did not move.

"What's going on?" Amber whispered.

At first, she thought Bagule was frozen, but then she noticed his arm still moved toward her, but slow. She lowered the shield then reached for the sword. A figure materialized behind Bagule. It was Aisha. She took the sword from Bagule's hand then smiled.

"Give that to me," Amber said.

"Why?" Aisha asked. "My aunt has no more reason to trust you with it than she does Bagule."

"Keep it then," Amber said. "As long as Bagule doesn't have it, I don't care who does. I just want to go home."

"Catch." Aisha tossed the sword to Amber. As soon as the hilt touched Amber's hand, Bagule's actions returned to normal. His hand slammed against Amber's shield and he grimaced in pain. Amber felt another surge of power as a connection formed between the sword and her necklace. Aisha stood beside her; Mansa Nyima blinked as control returned to her. They all glared at Bagule who backed away, holding his wounded hand.

"How did you . . .what happened?"

His eyes fell on Aisha.

"You! You did this!"

"She's the last person you need to worry about," Amber said.

Bagule's eyes went wide when he saw Amber coming toward him with the sword. He ran away as fast as he could. Amber began to pursue him but was stopped by a firm hand on her shoulder.

"Stop," the Mansa said. "There is no need to go after him."

"I have to end this," Amber said.

"No," Nyima said. "You have the necklace and Sonni Ali's sword. Nothing can stand against you. Not even me."

Amber watched Bagule as he ran to Nieleni. He knelt beside her, then lifted her into his arms. He glowered at Amber.

"This is not over, girl!"

Bagule waved his hand in a circular motion. The duo disappeared.

Amber's shoulders slumped as she lowered the sword and shield. She looked at Aisha and smiled.

"Thank you," she said.

Aisha shrugged. "I did want I had to do to get paid. Now let's go."

"Wait," Amber said.

Amber went to the Mansa, then extended the sword to her. "Here."

Nyima hesitated. "Are you sure?"

Amber nodded. "No one should have control over another against their will. Besides, I know you don't have any designs against Marai. Just make me one promise."

"What is that?" the Mansa asked.

"Do a better job at hiding it."

The Mansa took the sword, then held it against her chest.

"Thank you, Amber of Marai. You are a special girl."

Amber grinned. "I know."

"Come, Amber," Aisha said. "It's time. Your family has been waiting for a long time."

"What a minute," Amber said. "How are going to leave? There's no mirror."

Aisha drew a circle in the air. A shimmering space appeared similar to the mirror.

"I'm half djinn, remember?" Aisha said.

Aisha walked toward the portal, Amber following.

"Aisha," the Mansa said. "Promise me you'll return."

Aisha looked over her shoulder. "I'll consider it."

She stepped into the mirror and disappeared. Amber stepped up to the mirror the hesitated.

"This power I feel now, will it be this way from now on?"

Nyima smiled. "This is only the beginning. You have so much more to learn. Now go; your family waits for you."

Amber waved goodbye to Mansa Nyima then entered the portal.

CHAPTER THIRTY

Amber's journey through the portal this time was much more peaceful. After what seemed only a few seconds, she watched Aisha descend into her great grandfather's chamber. Amber did the same moments later and found herself surrounded by family. Aisha stood beside great grandfather, a smug look on her face. Everyone else seemed frozen in their emotions, eyeing her with wonder.

"My baby, my baby, my baby!" Mama screamed.

Mama jumped out of her chair, rushing Amber and wrapping her in her arms. Daddy was close behind hugging them both as he always did. Amber felt Mama's tears against her cheek and all the defenses she'd built up to deal with her time in the djinn Mansadom collapsed. She sobbed, holding her parents as tight as she could. When she was in the Mansadom, she didn't know if she would ever see them again. The nightmare of being held captive for hundreds of years stayed with her constantly. It took her all she had to focus on her situation and not fall into despair.

"I love you so much!" she said to them.

"We love you too, baby girl," Daddy replied.

"More than anything," Mama added.

"Amber."

Amber looked up into Grandma's face. She reluctantly let go of Mama and Daddy to hug her. Her embrace was gentler yet just as sincere.

"I'm so happy the Mansa set you free," she said.

Amber looked into her eyes. "How did you know? Did Aisha tell you?"

Grandma smiled. "I sensed it. I knew the Mansa would see your heart and release you. I didn't know how long that would take."

Grandma turned to Aisha.

"Thank you," she said.

"It's about time someone noticed I was here," Aisha replied.

Harriet entered the room then squealed

"Amby!"

Harriet ran to her then leaped. Amber caught her cousin and they fell to the floor.

"You're back! You're back!"

Amber giggled. "Yes I am. Now get off of me."

Harriet and Amber climbed back to their feet. Harriet clung to her, resting her head on her shoulder.

"I'm glad you didn't die," she said.

"Me, too," Amber replied.

Everyone's attention drifted to the chamber's entrance.

Bissau entered, his expression a mix of relief and guilt. He smiled weakly.

"Hello, Amber," he said.

Amber let go of Harriet and walked toward Bissau.

"Hey, Bissau."

They hugged, and it was different than any hug they ever shared. Amber closed her eyes and finally let her emotions go. She liked Bissau; she liked him a lot. She let her second sight go and it confirmed what she'd known for some time; Bissau liked her, too.

"I'm sorry I let this happen to you," he whispered.

"You couldn't prevent it," Amber replied.

"I was sent to protect you."

"You did the best you could, but I don't need your protection anymore. I just need your friendship."

Daddy ambled to them, placing a firm hand on Bissau's shoulder.

"That's enough hugging, Boy," he said. "Let my daughter go."

Bissau let Amber go. He stepped back then, bowed to Daddy.

"Forgive me," he said.

"I don't need all that," Daddy replied. "Just keep your distance."

"It's okay Daddy," Amber said. "Bissau's my friend. A good friend."

She looked at Bissau as she uttered those last words and his smile lit the room.

Great grandfather cleared his throat and drew everyone's attention.

"Amber, where is the sword?" he asked.

Amber approached her great grandfather.

"I gave it to Mansa Nyima, Baba."

Baba's eyes widened. "Was that wise?"

"The djinn means us no harm," Amber said. "They would never have been involved if Bagule had not dragged them into it."

"And what of Bagule?" Baba asked.

"He possessed the sword for a time, but I fought him for it. Thanks to Aisha, I defeated him."

Aisha shrugged. "You didn't need my help. It was you and your necklace. That charm is more powerful than any of you realize."

"Where are Bagule and Nieleni now?" Baba asked.

Amber lowered her head before answering. "I don't know."

"We won't have to worry about him anymore," Aisha commented. "This is twice Amber's defeated him. He should know by now."

"Bagule is determined," Baba said. "This is not the last we'll see of him and Nieleni."

"But for now, we will breathe easy," Grandma said.

"Yes," Baba replied.

Aisha gently moved Amber aside.

"Not that that's settled, I'll be collecting my pay."

Jakada nodded. "Bissau, please summon my servants."

Bissau nodded to Jakada. He shared a smile with Amber before leaving the chamber. He returned a few minutes later with the servants carrying Aisha's payment. She inspected the contents of the chests, then nodded.

"It's all here," she said.

She took a small bag of gold dust from the reward.

"This is all I need," she said. Baba's eyes went wide.

"Is that it?"

"Yes," Aisha replied. "I'm returning to Djinnland. All of this emotion has made me homesick."

Aisha walked to Amber, then leaned close to her.

"Take care of Bissau," she whispered. "He is a strong boy on the outside, but his heart his fragile."

"You be kind to your aunt," Amber said. "She loves you, and I know you love her, too."

Aisha hugged Amber, catching her off-guard. Amber hugged her back. Aisha stepped away, winked, then drew a portal. She scanned the room before jumping. Moments later the portal disappeared.

"Everyone, please come closer," Baba said. The family gathered close, Amber enjoying Mama's embrace.

"Amber, once again you have protected Marai," Baba said. "It is obvious the ancestors favor you. You came here as a girl unsure of her responsibilities, but now you are a woman of strength."

Baba turned his attention to Bissau.

"Bissau, I am proud of you. You have proven yourself as a warrior. You have given your all aiding and protecting my great granddaughter, and for this, you have my everlasting gratitude. I and Marai are in your debt."

Bissau bowed. "Thank you, Master Jakada. Your words humble me."

"I think Alake would agree with me in deciding that Amber no longer needs our supervision and advice. She has demonstrated that she is worthy to carry the title of Guardian of Marai."

Amber jerked, startled by Baba's words.

"What does that mean?" she asked.

"It means that Bissau's duties are complete."

Amber's eyes went to Bissau. Bissau continued to look at Baba, but his posture reflected the sadness of his colors.

"I have thought long on this," Baba said. "As much as I hate to admit it, I believe Bagule was right. Marai must no longer hide behind the Veil. We must open ourselves to the world. We have much to share with and learn from each other."

"Are you sure, Baba?" Grandma asked.

"Yes, Alake, I am," Baba replied. "I will discuss my decision with the Queen Mother and the Elders' council. I'm sure there will be some apprehension, but in the end my decision will prevail."

Baba sat on his stool. "Amber, Alake, and Bissau. Please step forward."

Amber slipped from Mama's arms and joined Grandma and Bissau before Baba.

"The people of Marai know nothing of the outside world," he said. "And the world knows nothing of us. I'm asking the three of you to act as ambassadors. Each of you have a different perspective of both worlds and together you are best to handle this enormous task."

"What does this mean for me, Master Jakada?" Bissau asked.

"You will remain in Atlanta, with Amber's permission," Baba said.

"I agree!" Amber blurted. Baba smiled.

"I thought you would," he said. "Alake, you will return with them as well. Your experience with both worlds exceeds all others."

"Yes, Baba," Grandma said. "As much as I've enjoyed my time in Marai, I do miss my family and my second home."

Baba looked over the three to Amber's family.

"Crystal and Sam, thank you for sharing your daughter with us. I know all of this has been difficult for you to comprehend, but you will in time. You come from a special family."

Mama's hand fell to her hips. "You're welcome, but it's not like you asked."

Amber rolled her eyes. "Mama!"

Baba laughed. "You're right, Crystal, we didn't. We ask for your forgiveness."

Baba turned his attention to Harriet.

"Harriet, it seems you share some talents with Amber."

Harriet ran forward. "I do!"

"I have something for you."

Jakada reached into his pocket and took out a necklace of lapis lazuli. Harriet scooted closer, allowing Baba to place the necklace around her neck.

"This will help you focus your powers," Jakada said. "Amber will show you as well."

Harriet ran her fingers over the gems then lunged for Baba, hugging him tight.

"Thank you, Baba!" she said.

"Don't knock him down, Harriet," Amber said.

"Oh yeah, right." Harriet released Baba, then returned to stand by Amber's parents.

Baba straightened his robes, then stood.

"If all minds are settled, I think it's time I returned you to your homes."

Baba rose from his stool then ambled to his mirror. He waved his hands across the surface and it swirled. After a few seconds, it cleared, revealing the interior of Amber's room.

Amber grasped Mama and daddy's hands. Harriet grabbed Mama's hand then nodded to Amber.

"Come on y'all," Amber said. "Let's go home."

Amber led her family to the mirror.

"One...two...three!" she said.

Together, they jumped through.

CHAPTER THIRTY-ONE

Amber sat in the guest room watching Harriet pack. Her parents were arriving soon, and Harriet waited until the last minute to gather everything. It had been a week since they returned from Marai and everyone was still dealing with what has occurred. Harriet seemed to handle it better than anyone else. The two of them were inseparable once they returned, bonded together now by more than just blood.

Harriet zipped her suitcase then plopped on the bed pouting.

"I don't want to go," she said."

"I don't want you to go, but you have to," Amber replied.

She went to the bed and sat beside Harriet. Harriet rested her head on Amber's shoulder.

"You're like my sister, Amby," she said.

"I feel the same," Amber said.

"Our parents only had one kid. What's up with that?"

Amber laughed. "Way too late to ask that question. It is what it is. We have each other, right?"

"Right!" Harriet said. She rolled her necklace between her fingers.

"Are you sure I can't tell Mama and Daddy about all this?"

"Not yet," Amber replied. "Grandma will decide when it's the right time."

"Okay," Harriet said. "I'm pretty good at keeping secrets."

"If you feel like you're about to break, text me," Amber told her. "We 'wizards have to stick together."

The doorbell rang and Amber felt a twinge of sadness.

"They're here," she said. "Let's go downstairs."

Amber grabbed Harriet's suitcase while Harriet slung her backpack over her shoulders. They walked side by side down the hallway; Amber took the lead as they decided the stairs. Uncle Jesse and Aunt Terry were in the foyer with Mama and Daddy, hugging and talking loudly. Aunt Terry looked up and a big smile filled her face.

"There's my baby!" she said.

Harriet ran by Amber and jumped into her mother's waiting arms.

"Where's my hug?" Uncle Jesse asked.

Harriet let her mother go and wrapped her father in a big hug.

"Did you have a good time?" Uncle Jesse asked.

"I had a great time," Harriet answered.

"What's this?" Aunt Terry asked.

Amber tensed as Aunt Terry touched Harriet's necklace.

"It's a souvenir," Harriet said.

"A souvenir? From Atlanta?" Aunt Terry laughed. "Girl you come here all the time."

"It's from the other place," Harriet said, then covered her mouth.

Aunt Terry's smile faded. "About that 'other place.' Y'all could have told somebody y'all were going to visit Mama. Better still, y'all could have told us Mama was back from Africa."

"That's my fault," Mama said. "She came back unexpectedly and we rushed down to Hilton Head to get her settled in. You and I can go down next week."

"Okay," Aunt Terry said.

"Well, we would visit, but we need to get back before dark," Uncle Jesse said. "Thank you for keeping Harriet. We'll have to return the favor."

"It was our pleasure," Daddy said. "We'll walk y'all out to the car."

Amber and her family followed Harriet and her parents to the car. Amber gave Harriet one more hug.

"Remember, text me anytime you need to talk," Amber said.

"I will Amby," Harriet said. "Love you!"

"Love you, too."

They watched the Harris family drive away before going back inside. Amber was about to climb the stairs when Daddy called out.

"Amber, your mother and I need to speak to you for a moment."

Amber froze as she did an inventory of what she could have done recently to make them angry. She shuffled into the family room. Mama and daddy sat together on the sofa; Amber sat in the loveseat.

"The past few weeks have been extraordinary," daddy said. "I'm still trying to understand it. Here we were thinking you were just struggling to adjust at Clifton. We had no idea."

"None at all," Mama said. "Well, at least until you threw that truck out of our way."

"What?" Daddy said.

"I'll tell you about later," Mama said. "Anyway, your daddy and I have been thinking, and we decided that if you want to leave Clifton Academy and enroll in Jackson High School, it's okay with us. You're a beautiful, intelligent, and apparently magical girl. You'll be amazing wherever you go."

Amber sprang to her feet.

"For real!"

Daddy laughed. "For real."

"I gotta tell Jasmine!"

Amber ran out of the family room and was halfway up the stairs before she stopped. She ran back down the stairs and hugged Mama and Daddy.

"Thank you! I love y'all so much!"

Amber ran to her room, grabbed her phone off the dresser and fell onto the bed, texting on the way down.

JASMINE!

What?

GUESS WHO'S TRANFERRING TO JACKSON HIGH?

NO!

YES!

Amber's phone vibrated and she answered the video call. Jasmine's face filled the screen.

"Guuuuurllll!"

They both screamed.

"I'm coming over," Jasmine said. "We'll go to Jazzy's for hamburgers and shakes. My treat!"

"Cool!"

Amber changed clothes, then hurried downstairs.

"Mama, Jasmine's coming to pick me up. Is that okay?"

"Yes," Mama said. "Next time ask before you tell her yes."

Jasmine pulled up a few minutes later and they were on their way."

"Hey, can we make a detour," Amber asked.

Jasmine looked at her suspiciously. "Where?"

"Bissau's place."

"I knew it," Jasmine said. "Well, if we're picking up Bissau, I'm texting Carlos to meet us."

"Okay," Amber said.

Jasmine's eyes went wide,

"You're not going to make fun of him?"

"No," Amber said. "Text Carlos when we get there."

Amber texted Bissau to meet them outside his complex. He was there when they pulled up, smartly dressed as always. He opened the back door and climbed inside.

"Hello Jasmine," he said.

"Hey Bissau," Jasmine replied. "I hope I said your name right."

"You did."

Bissau touched Amber's shoulder.

"Hello, Amber."

She turned to look into his eyes.

"Hey, Bissau."

The car was quiet as they drove to Jazzy's, the tension between Amber and Bissau hanging in the air. Jasmine maneuvered the car into the small parking space. Carlos was waiting, waving at them as they pulled up. Amber shook her head.

"I just don't see it," she said.

"Shut it," Jasmine replied. "He's my boyfriend. You don't need to see it."

Jasmine, Amber and Bissau got out of the car. Jasmine trotted to Carlos and kissed him on the cheek before they went inside. Bissau headed for the door behind them.

"Bissau, wait," Amber said.

Bissau turned to face her.

"What is it, Amber?" he said.

"I need to talk to you for a minute."

Bissau came closer and Amber tried her best not to shake.

"Yes?"

"When I was a captive of the djinn, I thought I wouldn't see anyone again. I thought I'd never see you again."

Bissau smiled. "I knew I would see you again. I wasn't going to stop looking for you until I found you."

Amber moved closer to him.

"I decided if I became free, I would never neglect the people I care about. I would keep them close and always let them know how I feel. So, the thing is, I like you, and not just like a friend. I . . . I think you should be my boyfriend."

Amber closed her eyes and extended her hand toward Bissau. After what seemed like forever, he took it.

"Nothing would make me happier," he said. "I've wanted to tell you how I felt for so long, but I didn't think it was my place. So now that I'm your boyfriend, what do we do?"

"I don't know," Amber replied. "I've never had a boyfriend before."

"Let's go inside and ask Jasmine and Carlos," Bissau said. "I'm sure Jasmine will have tons of advice."

Bissau and Amber laughed together. Bissau's face became serious.

"What do you see?" he asked.

Amber looked at their hands. They both were lavender.

"We match," she said.

Amber kissed Bissau on the cheek, and they walked into Jazzy's together.

END

ABOUT THE AUTHOR

Milton J. Davis is a Black Fantastic fiction writer and owner of MVmedia, LLC, a publishing company specializing in Science Fiction, Fantasy based on African/African Diaspora culture, history, and traditions. Milton is the author of nineteen novels; his most recent is the post-apocalyptic adventure *Gunman's Peace*. He is the editor and co-editor of nine anthologies; *The City, Terminus, Blacktastic, Dark Universe* with Gene Peterson; *Griots: A Sword and Soul Anthology* and *Griot: Sisters of the Spear*, with Charles R. Saunders; *The Ki Khanga Anthology,* the *Steamfunk! Anthology*, and the *Dieselfunk anthology* with Balogun Ojetade. MVmedia has also published *Once Upon A Time in Afrika* by Balogun Ojetade and *Abegoni: First Calling* and *Nyumbani Tales* by

Sword and Soul creator and icon Charles R. Saunders. Milton's work had also been featured in *Black Power: The Superhero Anthology*; Skelos *2: The Journal of Weird Fiction and Dark Fantasy Volume 2, Steampunk Writers Around the World* published by Luna Press and *Bass Reeves Frontier Marshal Volume Two*. His Steamfunk story The Swarm was nominated for the 2017 British Science Fiction Award. You can contact Milton Davis from his website: https://www.miltonjdavis.com

For more books by Milton J. Davis and other exciting titles, visit MVmedia, www.mvmediaatl.com, for the Best in Black Speculative Fiction

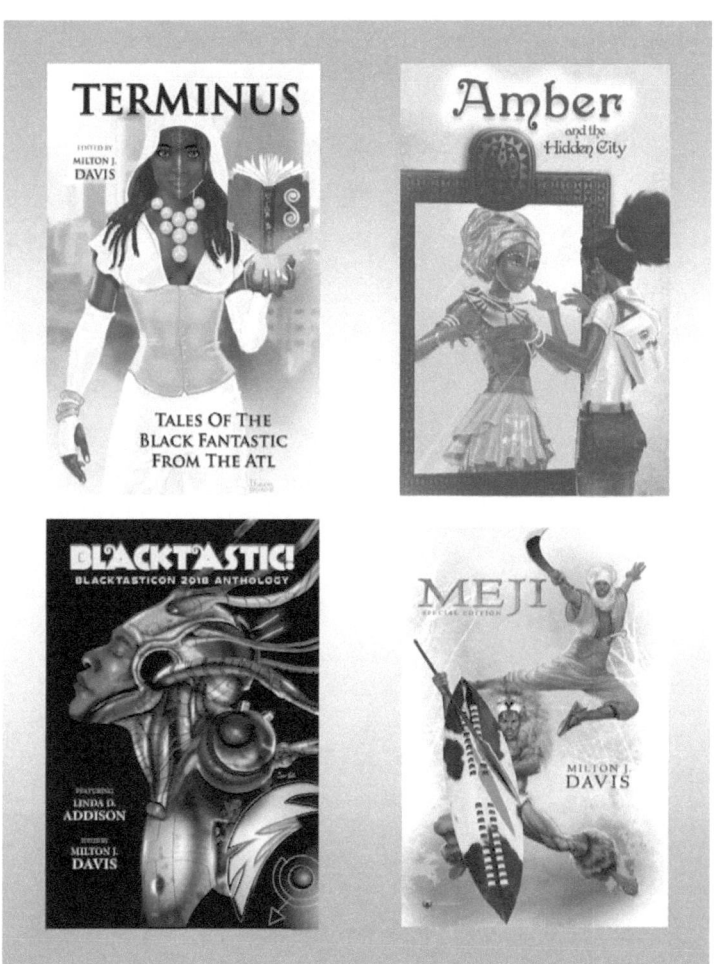